Portrait

Figure 1 The Elderly Daniel Boone Hunting in Missouri by Alonzo Chappel (c. 1861). With permission of the Library of Congress.

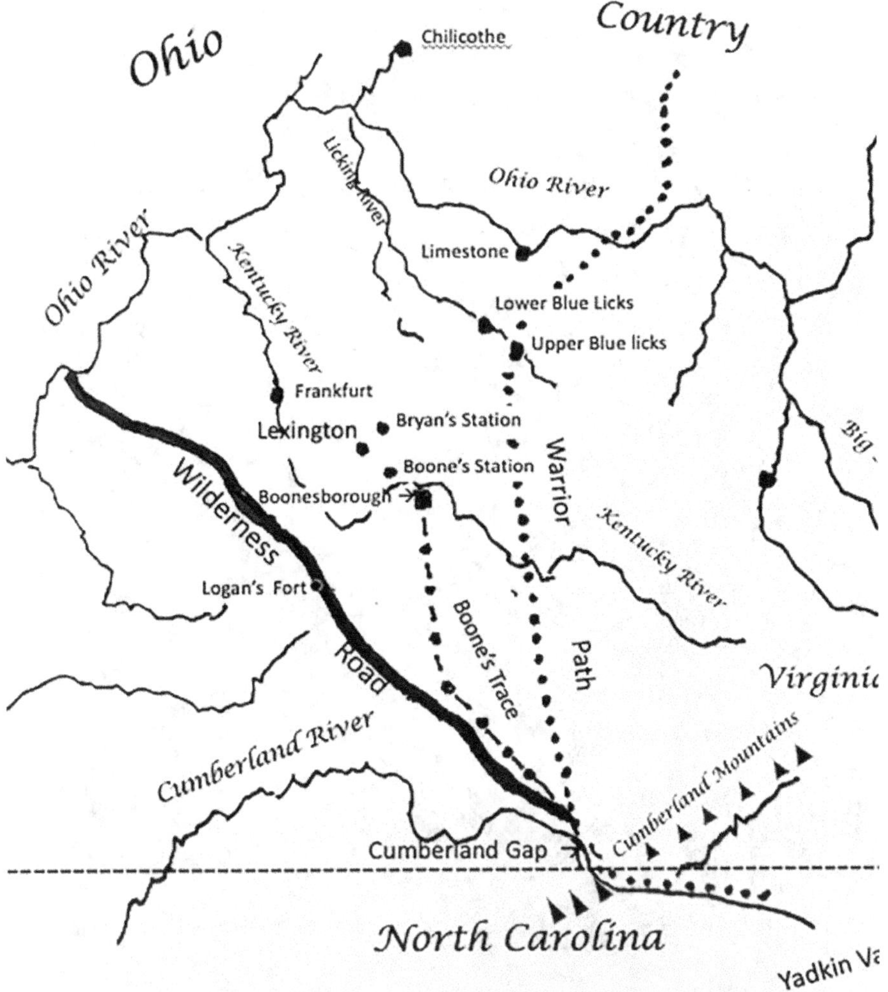

Figure 2 Author's map of the eastern Kentucky Territory, during the time of Daniel Boone. Based on a map from Boone: A Biography by Robert Morgan.

Figure 3 Fort Boonesborough, based on descriptions of the fort and drawings: https://explorekyhistory.ky.gov/files/show/3930; https://www.wisconsinhistory.org/Records/Image/IM24939, https:// explorekyhistory.ky.gov/files/show/1862; https://en.wikipedia.org/ wiki/File:Old_Fort_at_Boonesborough,_1775.jpg

Daniel Boone and Me

Daniel Boone and Me

Noelle A. Granger

Dedication

Dedicated to the remarkable hunter and explorer, Daniel Boone, to the American Indians sadly pushed from their lands by the inexorable westward migration of European immigrants, and finally in recognition of the grit and determination of the women settlers of Kentucky.

Table of Contents

Figures

Chapter 1
The Worst Day of My Life

When the Shawnee attacked our home in Kentucky that early summer day, my parents pushed me and my four-year-old brother Thatcher into the root cellar, a dug-out space beneath our cabin floorboards. "Stay there even if it gets quiet," my mother had said with a shaky voice. "And don't make a sound." I then heard her drag the bed over the floorboards.

When Thatch started to whimper, I covered his mouth with my hand, even though it made it harder for him to breathe. After some gunfire, I heard the sounds of struggles, groans, a thump, and my mother's screams. Then came noises of a ransacking, with soft footsteps padding here and there. Finally, it became quiet, and Thatch ceased to struggle…until flames crackled overhead and he started to cry out in fear. Our home was on fire!

I laid on top of Thatch to keep him from burning, as hot, woody smoke filled our hiding place. I could feel the heat from the flames on my back, and we both coughed from the smoke. I said a prayer begging God to keep the fire from spreading into the cellar and to keep us alive. I hoped it would be over soon, as my back hurt badly from the flames above us.

Once the crackling had died down, I could hear nothing more. Despite the heat, Thatch and I shivered with fright, and we stayed there, keeping quiet beneath the floor, until we both fell asleep. Thatch woke me sometime later, whispering he was hungry. Ma had stored some dried apples in a sack in the cellar, and I emptied the contents of the sack, jamming as many as I could in the pocket of my apron.

Thatch grabbed two and bit into the biggest one. I hastily ate another. Still hearing no sounds, I decided it might be safe to get out of the hole, but I had to push hard to lift away what remained of the floorboards and the remnants of the bed. "Don't you dare come up just yet, Thatch," I told him, shoving his head down as I climbed out. I knew what I would find would be horrible.

When I saw the burned bodies of my parents, I gagged. I could barely tell they had been Ma and Pa, shreds of their burnt clothes sticking to what was left of their bodies and my mother's beautiful long auburn hair almost gone. It was the hardest thing of my short life not to scream from the horror of it. I turned away and threw up the apple I'd eaten.

They're dead! What am I to do? I stood, not moving, shaking and crying.

I quieted my sobs, thinking I couldn't let Thatch see this. Dragging some charred wood to where they lay, I covered their bodies to hide them as best I could from my brother's eyes. My parents had told me many times of the dangers all around us and had warned me such a day might come. Since I was six years older than Thatch, they'd made me promise to take care of my brother, and that promise gave me strength, despite the sickness that threatened to make me heave again.

Having finished his apples, Thatch started whining that he wanted to climb out. I turned away from the bodies, gritted my teeth, and said, "Come on up. But mind where you're putting your feet." I pulled him up out of the hole, placing myself between him and what was left of our parents.

"You go on out there," I pointed towards our field, "and see if you can find Bessie or Scout or any of our chickens." Thatch loved our cow and horse and especially the chickens and went straightaway with only a brief look around.

With Thatch in the field, I could let my tears come. Rummaging around in the remains of our home for anything useful, I found some scorched bread. I put that in my pockets along with the rest of the apples. I wiped my eyes on the sleeve of my dress as I left the ruins of the house and went out to find Thatch. He stood in our burned cornfield, looking around. "Bessie and Scout are gone, Liza. The chickens, too. Did the Indians take them? Where are Ma and Pa? Did they run away?"

"You ask too many questions. I expect those Indians took 'em. Ma and Pa musta run into the forest. They told me if the Indians came, once we were sure they'd left, we should walk to the fort. I'll bet they're already heading to the fort for help. I just need to find the trail Pa showed me." My heart twisted as I lied to Thatch, but I just couldn't tell him, not right then. He had to be strong for the long walk to the fort.

Everything my folks had told me rattled around in my head, and I couldn't seem to figure out where that stupid trail was. Thinking on those bodies made it worse. I tried hard to recollect which way Pa and me had gone on the one trip I'd taken to the fort nearly a year ago. On shaky legs, I searched the woods at the far end of the cornfield until I found it.

"Over here, Thatch. I can't barely make it out, but this trail seems to be heading in the right direction." I took his hand, and we began a trek through the woods that went on for the rest of that day, stopping only to drink from a tiny stream and to rest when Thatch got tired.

When darkness hid the trail, Thatch asked, "Can I sleep now, Liza? It's dark and scary, and my legs are tired. And I'm hungry. Please?"

I reminded myself how short Thatch's legs were, how hard he had to work to keep up with me, even though I'd taken smaller steps. He had to be done in. "Sure, let's rest here for the night. See that big mountain laurel over there? We can crawl under it to sleep. Let's eat something first."

We sat down on the forest floor, and I gave him some of the bread and apples, but he slumped over asleep after three bites. I finished his apple and a small piece of the bread, then carried him over to the bush. Pushing him as far under it as I could, I crawled in alongside him. The air had become chilly after the sun set, so I wrapped myself around his little body to provide him some warmth. I tried to stay awake, my ears straining to hear any sounds. But before long, my eyes shut, too, and I didn't feel my scorched back.

When I awoke with the rising sun, the memory of what had happened the day before hit me like a hammer. I lay there quietly on my side, tears leaking down the sides of my face onto the ground. Finally, I wiped my tears and poked Thatch because we needed to get going. He awoke tired and whining, like the little boy he was.

After we ate the last of the bread and more dried apples, Thatch said, "I can see your back Liza, where your dress is burnt away. It's red and peeling. Does it hurt?"

It did hurt, a little more than the day before, but I smiled and said, "Not much. Are you finished? We need to get going."

We picked up the trail again, lost it, backtracked, then found it.

"Why do we keep going back, Liza? We walked this way before."

"I'm doing my best, Thatch. I know you're tired, but we have to keep going. Please," I pleaded.

I wondered if I could keep him walking until we reached the fort. I couldn't get rid of the sight of Ma's and Pa's bodies, but I had to keep Thatch from fearing the Indians might be tracking us. So I talked quietly to him, trying to remember the bedtime stories Ma had told us.

By midmorning, Thatch seemed to recover from the shock of the previous day and asked a lot of questions as we walked along.

"Where are Ma and Pa? Why did the Indians burn our house down? Can I have an apple? Can we stop and rest for a while? When will we be there?"

I couldn't get him to shush, and his voice got high and loud. Finally. I promised him a meal of chicken and corn pudding when we got to the fort, if he'd only shush.

He smiled but kept up his chatter. When Thatch's legs got too tired to carry him, I put him on my back, despite the pain. When the shadows grew shorter as the sun passed overhead, I had to stop and chose a cleared area under a loblolly pine. It felt like heaven to have Thatch off my raw back.

We'd only been sitting for a few minutes when I heard the faint sound of a twig snapping. Indians! Putting my hand over my brother's mouth, I whispered, "Someone's following us. We need to run!" Grabbing his hand, I yanked him up and ran as fast as we could. We were soon out of breath, which kept him from talking.

The faint sound of rushing water reminded me that Pa and I had crossed a river on our trip. "There's a river up ahead," I whispered to Thatch. "We can use it to hide our footsteps." Pa had taught me to walk in the water to hide our tracks. The river ran at the bottom of a steep hill, and we started down together, holding hands, slipping and sliding on the leaves and pebbles. At the bottom of the hill, I could hear a waterfall. "Come on, Thatch! I have an idea."

We stumbled and tripped over slippery rocks and roots along the water's edge, and I finally had to carry him again. Sweating and out of breath when we finally came to the shining curtain of water, I put Thatch down and eagerly stepped into its spray. "Don't be afraid," I said. "Doesn't this feel just fine?" I stepped through the falling drops and pulled him into the space behind it. The water soothed my back where my calico dress had burned through. "There. Just like a cold bath. Wasn't that fun?" When he nodded, I whispered, "Don't make a sound now," and held my fingers to his lips. I gave him the one last apple I'd hidden in my apron, hoping his eating would stop his questions.

A short while later, we saw a dark figure through the water's curtain, moving slowly across it. I pulled Thatch to where I sat on a small rock and, hugging him, made us into as tight a ball as possible. Thinking of what could happen to us sent me to shaking. *We'll be captured! I'm sorry, Pa.*

With those fears pounding through me, I barely heard a man's voice over the sound of the falling water, "Eliza, Thatcher—I know you're in there. I've been tracking you since yesterday. Come on out. You're safe now. I'll take you to the fort."

I knew that voice—it was our neighbor, Colonel Daniel Boone.

And that's how Daniel Boone rescued us.

Chapter 2

Where Will Thatch and Me Find a Home?

After he found us on that terrible day, he took us to the fort named after him, Boonesborough. He carried Thatch most of the way and held my hand when the trail was wide enough. The fort was in the middle of a big meadow, with a river running by it a little distance away. We entered the fort through a tall gate made of straight posts, set into a high wall, which Colonel Boone called a palisade. Two men guarded the gate, and they called out greetings to the colonel as we passed through.

"Glad to see you found them kids, Colonel."

"Welcome back."

"You see any Indians?"

Inside the palisade I could see a large, square space, about as big as my pa's acre of corn. Single-story log cabins ran along the sides with bigger houses—I later learned they were called blockhouses—at each of the front corners. Another gate, closed, stood in the middle of the back wall, and nobody seemed to be standing watch there.

Three cabins sat in the middle of the open space. Colonel Boone told us one was his home, another his gun shop, and the third belonged to a Colonel Callaway. Cows and horses stood tied down or roamed here and there among plenty of people and chickens. After living in a single cabin with no neighbors, I thought Boonesborough sure had a lot of folks. Thatch and I almost tripped over ourselves with our heads turning this way and that.

"Rebecca," Colonel Boone called when we got to the door to his house. "We got visitors."

"This is my wife, Rebecca," he told us, as a woman near as tall as Colonel Boone came through the door, wiping her hands on her apron. She had lovely dark hair with streaks of grey and dark, piercing eyes, which looked me and Thatch up and down. "These here must be the Corey children. You can tell me later how you found them." The sound of children laughing came from behind her. "You must be hungry about now. Come in and I'll find you something to eat."

We both charged the door at the same time, and Colonel Boone laughed when neither of us could get in side by side. "Take your time. I might could use some food, too, wife."

After the bright sun outside, the inside of the cabin seemed pretty dark. In a moment or so we could see the children. "Eliza, Thatcher, meet Susannah, Jemima, Levina—she looks to be your age, Eliza — then Rebecca, little Daniel, Jesse and William." Mrs. Boone gestured towards the group.

"Howdee," said Susannah, who looked to be the oldest. The rest of the children just stared. For the first time, I thought what Thatch and I might look like to them, me with my burnt dress and tangled hair, and both of us with faces that had never been dirtier.

A little boy who looked like he'd just learned to walk staggered over to us and grabbed my leg to keep from falling.

"That's Jesse. He likes people," said Susannah. "And that's William over there in the crib. He's just born."

I walked over and looked down at his little red face. "You sure have a lot of young'uns," I said.

"Oh, this ain't all." Mrs. Boone said with some sadness in her voice. "Israel will join us tonight. He's out hunting with Susanna's husband, Captain Hays."

"Children, take the little ones outside. Eliza, Thatcher, sit." Mrs. Boone went to the hearth and ladled something steaming into two bowls. I almost fainted from the wonderful smell when she placed the bowls in front of us on the table. "Rabbit stew, eat up!" She didn't have to repeat that order. Thatch and I gobbled it down, and Colonel Boone ate his stew almost as quickly.

After eating, Mrs. Boone gave us a bucket of water and a rag so we could clean ourselves up, then came back with a pot of some sort of salve for my back, which she spread ever so gently. I welcomed the soothing feel of it. Then, my belly being full and feeling the warmth and safety of the Boone's home, I allowed thoughts of the day before slip back into my head. The horrible emptiness of knowing that Ma and Pa had died returned and tears came again.

Thatch, who as yet didn't know they were gone, started to cry with me. "'Liza, I want Ma and Pa. I want to go home. Where are they?" he sobbed.

Mrs. Boone came over to the table and sat between us, putting an arm around each us. "There, there, Thatcher," she soothed, pulling a handkerchief from her apron pocket and wiping his tears. Then she handed the handkerchief to me. "Eliza, you and your brother have experienced more than any child should have to. You can cry all you want, until you are cried out. If you want to talk to me about it, that's fine. The colonel, too. But try to think about the good times you had with your ma and pa. That'll see you through. You're brave and you're strong, remember that."

We both leaned into her, Thatch, not understanding what she'd said, whimpered. He soon fell asleep, and my eyes started to droop.

I remember being carried to a straw mattress and having a blanket tucked around me, nothing more.

The next morning I woke with a start, not remembering where I was. When I did, the memory hit me so hard I fell back on the mattress and just lay there, empty, not knowing what to do. Finally, when I looked around the room, I saw Mrs. Boone, stirring something in a pot over the fire.

"Eliza, I'm glad you're wake. You slept a long time. Get yourself up and have some porridge. That'll start you off real good." Mrs. Boone's reassuring voice got me out of bed.

"Where's Thatch?" I asked.

"Oh, he's outside with the children. Probably chasing chickens."

"He's good at that."

I drifted through the rest of the day, trying to help out where I could, grinding corn, sweeping the floor, airing the blankets.

That evening, after our meal, Colonel Boone asked us to sit outside with him. The air was warm and, truthfully, a bit stinky with all the people and animals living within the fort. I missed the clean air of our farm.

Colonel Boone sat on a chunk of tree trunk, and we sat at his feet.

Thatch, who had not spoken a word of what had happened to us, suddenly asked, "Where are Ma and Pa? I want to see my ma and pa. Are they here?"

"Son," replied the colonel, carefully sorting his words, "they have gone to meet their Maker. They'll see you again someday, but they are no longer among us."

Thatch's face crumpled and he began to cry. "We can't see them again? Who is the Maker? Is that God?"

I started to cry right along with him.

Mrs. Boone, who had quietly come outside and had sat down in the door to the cabin, recognized that Thatch understood about God and told him, "Yes, they're with God now. You can pray to them each night and keep them in your heart, where they will always be." She stood and gathered a sobbing Thatch into her arms and wiped his tears.

After a while, when Thatch had quieted and I had wiped my tears on my sleeve, Colonel Boone asked, giving me a squinted look, "Eliza, do you know of any kin of your ma and pa. Brothers? Sisters?"

I thought for a minute. "Ma and Pa did tell us some about their families. They live in a place called Con-e-ti-cut, but I don't remember their names. They were in our family Bible but that burned up with the house. Do you think you could find some Coreys in Con-e-ti-cut?"

"That's a mighty big place," relied the colonel. "Bigger than Kentucky with many more people. I'm not sure how we'd do that."

I had started to cry again, wondering what would happen to me and Thatch, when he said, "If you're content here, then Rebecca and I would like you to stay with us."

Mrs. Boone added, "The house is small, but we can always manage more children…if you think you'd be happy with us."

I just sat there, thinking about their offer and looking at Thatch. *Staying with the Boones would be the best for my brother…and me.*

"So you think you might be content here?" asked Mrs. Boone.

"No!" Thatch began to scream, much worse than his crying. "I want to go home!"

I hugged him and whispered," Thatch, our farm is gone. Ma and Pa, too." My voice broke, but I took a deep breath and kept talking. "The Boones are nice people and they'll take care of us. And I'll never leave you." I held him until he'd quieted, realizing our lives were going to be very different from that day on. I nodded to Mrs. Boone and felt relief that I'd no longer have to worry about what would happen to us and being solely responsible for Thatch.

"Eliza," Mrs. Boone said, "I'm sure your ma taught you lots about the work she did every day."

Even though my eyes burned with held-back tears and I ached for my parents, I knew I owed the Boones whatever I could do in return for taking us in. "Yes, Ma'am. I can cook some, wash clothes, tend a garden, milk a cow, and she was just learning me to spin wool. Oh, and I can knit."

Mrs. Boone smiled. "Then you'll fit right in. Thatcher, you're getting to be a big boy. You can help mind Jesse and William, along with the chickens."

Thatch's eyes lit up. While I wasn't so sure he could mind the youngest Boones, he was pretty gentle collecting eggs, so I knew he'd be gentle with Jesse and William.

Over the next few weeks, Thatch and I became a part of the large Boone family. At first, we often cried together, especially when we saw something that reminded us of Ma and Pa—the men working in the cornfields, Mrs. Boone leaning over a kettle in the fireplace—but there was plenty to see and do. Mrs. Boone kept us busy, and although she had to scold Thatch about chasing the chickens, she praised him outrageously when he found their eggs. Thatch also took good care of Jessie and rocked baby William when he fretted.

Mrs. Boone paid especial attention to Thatch. I thanked her for it, and it was then that she told me Thatch reminded her a little of their first son, James. Two years before, along the Wilderness Trail, a band of Shawnees, Delawares and Cherokees had attacked James and the party he led, consisting of four other men and two slaves. James had become lost while attempting to catch up with his father and the settlers Colonel Boone was guiding to Kentucky. James had been killed in the attack, and the Boones still felt the sadness of his loss.

One day, Colonel Boone took two horses so he and I could ride back to my family's homestead and bury Ma and Pa. The trip took less time than the way Thatch and I had taken when we ran from the house. When we got there, the colonel tethered the horses and sent me out to the fields to see if any corn remained and to the vegetable garden to gather anything left—carrots, potatoes, beans, and squash. While I did this, he buried what was left of my parents.

When he'd finished, he called me to the burial site explaining, "I put a mound of stones on their graves to keep the wild animals away and to let you know where they're buried." We said the Lord's Prayer and then he left me to say my own good-byes.

"Ma and Pa, I hope you can hear me. We're living safe with Colonel and Mrs. Boone. I promise I will always take care of Thatch, no matter what. When he's growed, we can take care of each other. I miss you so much." I wiped the tears from my eyes and walked away to rejoin the colonel.

"Let's put the stuff you gathered in these sacks," he said, "and see if there is anything of use left in the house." I found a few scorched pans where the hearth had been, and I discovered Ma's locket while digging around in the charred wood. Inside I found pictures of her pa and ma, who looked very much like her. I figured this would help me remember what she looked like. Already my memories had become blurred around the edges.

As we rode away, I felt the door to my early life had closed forever.

ᘓ   ᘔ

Colonel Boone's appearance, not to mention his stories, completely captured my little brother's attention. When we first met him, Colonel Boone had long braided hair, dressed with bear grease. He tied his long shirt with a leather belt, from which hung a powder horn, a bullet pouch, a knife and a tomahawk. Not so different from our pa. But Pa wore breeches, while Colonel Boone dressed himself like an Indian in a breechclout—a length of cloth that passed between the legs and then under a cloth belt, with the extra cloth hanging in the front and behind. Breechclouts were not so unusual since we often saw them on hunters who came to the fort. Colonel Boone also wore long leggings pulled above the knee and held in place by straps, and he had moccasins on his feet.

Most nights, with only the fire in the fireplace giving light to the room, the colonel, if asked, would tell us about his life. Although his own children had heard much of what he told us, they still listened or fell asleep where they sat.

Early on, Thatch started in on one of his flood of questions. "Who are your ma and pa, Colonel Boone?"

"Well, I were born in Pennsylvania in 1734. My pa was a weaver and Ma ran a dairy. She did the milking and made butter, and I helped her herd the cows. Until I discovered I'd rather be hunting and exploring in the forests nearby. That didn't improve her temper one bit." He chuckled at the thought.

I did a quick subtraction in my head, proud that in addition to teaching me how to read, Ma had learned me how to add and subtract numbers. I figured out he was forty- one. He was *old*.

"Do you have any brothers and sisters, Colonel Boone?"

Here we go.

"I have ten brothers and a sister, least the last time I knew. We moved to Carolina when I were seventeen. I'd already took some long hunts into the western country, what people called this place back then, before we even moved. Didn't make it to Kentucky, though, not then."

"How come you have so many brothers and sisters?" asked Thatch.

"Thatch," I whispered, "you don't ask questions like that."

"That's okay, young'uns. Maybe because we were Quakers? No idea."

"Did you go to school?" Thatch just couldn't help himself.

Another deep chuckle. "Not so you'd call it schooling. Me and school just didn't get along. My sister taught me to read, though."

"Are you going to make us go to school?"

Colonel Boone laughed. "There ain't no school here, leastways not yet."

Thatch looked pleased.

I later discovered that Mrs. Boone couldn't read nor write, nor could any of their children. I vowed to help the youngest two with that but wondered if the older ones would have any interest.

As Thatch's eyes started to close that night, Mrs. Boone told us all it was past time to go to bed. The children crowded the cabin, but somehow everyone had a place to rest their head, sleeping in any space available on ticking stuffed with corn husks or straw, or on soft pine boughs covered with a blanket. Adding to the sleeping family were Susanna Boone and her husband, William Hayes. Susanna, now fifteen, would soon have their first child.

Chapter 3
Everyone Hunts—Even Me

Despite this crowded house, Mrs. Boone kept a tidy home, fed everyone, and managed to provide us with clothing. She gave me a dress to replace the one with the burned-out back, one that Jemima had outgrown. Made of course-spun flax with a high neck and narrow sleeves, it fit me well enough. I watched her piece some cloth from a worn-out shirt over the back of my old blue dress, so I had two. I also got a shift to wear underneath it and a straw bonnet with a large brim to keep off the sun.

The Boone's crowded and busy home provided just the medicine Thatch and I needed to adjust to life without our parents, but I worried that there wouldn't be enough food. Would we be put out on our own when that happened? We still thought Indians could attack us at any time, and both of us feared leaving the safety of the fort.

Probably eighty people lived in the fort—free men, some slaves, boys, but only a few women and girls. Most of the men had claimed land in areas around the fort and worked their land, just as my parents had done— planting crops, harvesting, or hunting, depending on the season. I often worried when I saw that among all these people, no one took charge of guarding the back gate of the fort and only sometimes did a guard stand at the front one.

One morning, after me and Levina, who was going on ten like me, had finished a considerable amount of washing and had hung the clothes to dry, Colonel Boone himself approached me. He carried a long rifle crosswise in his arms.

"Eliza," he said, "my wife knows how to hunt and she's a dead shot. All my children know how to hunt, so I think you should too. You have to be able to take care of yourself and Thatch, especially if anything should happen to me or Rebecca."

Levina, who stood beside me, nodded. "I can shoot and I got me some rabbits not long ago."

"I've gone hunting with my pa," I replied, "but he never showed me how to shoot."

"So come with me now. And leave your bonnet here."

Levina gave me a friendly push. "You go on with Pa."

I followed his long strides across the meadow outside the fort, past the corn and vegetable patches, and into the dense, surrounding woods. My moccasins let me walk without making much noise. The colonel had showed me how make my skirts less of a bother when I had to walk through the bushes, by bunching them up into my belt front and back, making them like pants.

"Are we hunting a deer today, Colonel Boone?" I whispered, loud enough for him to hear me.

He responded with that chuckle of his. "Whenever you hunt deer, the hardest part is finding them. So we'll just see what's out here. Maybe rabbits."

We spent some time scouting, with the colonel checking for tracks and other signs and showing me what he saw. I knew he was very skilled at this, and I vowed to learn the signs myself. He showed me some bear scat, a pile of large black turds big as Colonel Boone's foot. Rabbit scat looked different, small round droppings, and when we found a clearing with a lot of it, we stopped.

"I'm going to show you how to load the rifle, Eliza, so pay attention," he said quietly. He stood the rifle on its stock and took the powder horn from his belt, uncorking it and pouring some powder into the barrel of the rifle.

"How do you know how much powder to put in?" I lowered my voice, too.

"I don't know, I just do. I'll show you the right amount later." Then he plugged the powder horn back up and took a small piece of greasy cloth from his bag along with a lead ball. Wrapping the ball in the scrap of cloth, he pushed it into the barrel. Then he slid out a long rod from a holder on the side of the rifle and used it to push the ball down into the barrel. "You have to push hard on this ramrod to make sure you've got the ball all the way down, girl." Then he lifted the rifle and half-cocked the firing pin, which made a clicking sound. A small amount of powder then went into the pan in front of the firing pin. "You got to light this powder to get the rifle to fire," he explained.

"How?"

"See here, this piece that looks like a hammer? It holds a flint. When I pull the trigger, the flint strikes this piece of metal in front of it and creates a spark. The spark lights the powder in the pan and then the gun goes off."

"This all seems pretty hard, Colonel Boone." I frowned.

"You're right, but you're a smart girl, you'll learn. Mind, it takes some time to reload for another shot. That's the problem with these darn rifles. Now, let's get down on the ground. I'll prop the rifle up for you, and I want you to pull the hammer all the way back. When you see a rabbit, sight it along the barrel and pull the trigger."

I did as he told me, with the stock resting against my shoulder, but I got nervous, fearing I would mess things up. I practiced sighting along the barrel. We waited, breathing quietly. After a right long time, a rabbit hopped into view. I got him in my sight, but my hand shook as I pulled the trigger. The push back from the rifle shot hurt my shoulder, surprising me. I'm not sure if I was more surprised or hurt. And I missed the rabbit.

"You have to keep a steady arm, Eliza. But you'll get another chance. Right now we gotta move on. All those rabbits have hightailed it."

We had to walk a ways to find another bunch of rabbit scat. This time, I reloaded the rifle by myself and spread out on the ground, elbows fixed firmly. I took a deep breath and held my whole self steady, feeling I could do this and knowing there'd be a kick to my shoulder. I could hardly believe it when I hit a rabbit!

"You did well, Eliza," said Colonel Boone. "You're going to make a good hunter."

I beamed with pride. I couldn't have felt better if my pa had said it. By the end of the day, we had five rabbits, including two I'd nailed. "Are deer a lot harder to shoot, Colonel Boone?"

"Yessiree. And harder to find. We'll do some deer hunting this winter on our usual trek."

During the following months, I learned a lot more about tracking and eventually became a good shot, often bringing back rabbits and other small animals for the pot. I once made a mistake and brought back a polecat, both of us stinking to high heavens. Mrs. Boone was not particularly pleased and had me wash thoroughly in a large barrel of water.

Despite my new skill, I remained very afraid of running into Indians, so I always asked someone with experience to come with me when I hunted.

In October, the whole family, even the little ones, packed up and went on what Colonel Boone called their winter hunt. We roamed the far reaches of western Kentucky, hunting deer and bear, and I got better at reading tracks. The quiet of the forests and the wide open spaces tasted of freedom, and I understood why the colonel loved roaming.

Whenever we stopped for a few days, he had us build a three-sided lean-to and cover it with brush. The open side faced the fire. In the evenings, we'd fill our bellies with meat from the animals we'd shot, along with the biscuits Mrs. Boone made over the fire. We learned to sleep on a bed of hemlock branches or piles of dried leaves, with our feet to the fire to keep them warm.

That weren't to say this trek was a fun adventure. Many times, we were wet and chilled to the bone by the time we found a place to hole up for a day or two. We slogged through piles of snow, and my feet darn near froze before I could get dry socks on. The little ones often whined, and poor Mrs. Boone spent a lot of time tending to them, in addition to cooking and trying to keep us dry. Thatch tried to help, but he liked trailing after Colonel Boone a lot more.

When I shot my first deer, I discovered I didn't much like the gutting and skinning of it. When I'd finished and washed my hands and arms off in a nearby stream of icy water, the colonel told me, "We gotta hoppus your deer back to camp."

"Hoppus? What does that mean?" I asked. *What a strange word!*

"It's how we carry deer carcasses."

I watched as he tied the front and rear legs on each side of my deer together, making straps out of the legs. Putting his arms through the tied legs, he hefted the deer onto his back. "When you're older and stronger, you can do this yourself."

I just watched in wonder.

During evenings around the fire, as we warmed ourselves, I learned a lot more about Colonel Boone. As he told Thatch and me, "After my family moved to the province of North Carolina, I decided I wanted to settle somewhere in the western territories. Carolina had too many people and I like to hunt alone. So I headed out into the mountains. On one of those trips, I found a trail made by buffalo and Indians through a place called the Cumberland Gap, and that trail brought me to the place that is now called Kentucky. By the time settlers took that route, they called it the Wilderness Trail. I know your parents came to Kentucky that way, too."

He had a lot of interesting stories about his early treks into the western mountains, but some of those stories scared me.

"There was a winter," he told us one evening, "I think in the mountains of Tennessee, when some Cherokees surrounded me. I became their prisoner. Couldn't blame them—I was hunting in their territory. Their leader gave me a name—Wide Mouth." He smiled at the memory. "Probably because I talked so much."

As usual, Thatch, wide-eyed, hung on every word of the story. "Then what happened?"

"Well, since I couldn't leave, I welcomed them and shared my whiskey with them. I've found if you're respectful and look at them direct, they tend to treat you the same. So they let me go. But not before they took all the furs I'd collected in their territory."

I had to ask him, "Have you seen any Indian sign around here?"

"Yup, but their trail headed south."

"You're sure of that?"

He raised an eyebrow. Nevertheless, Colonel Boone's rifle always stood primed and ready, and I thought a lot about what would happen if Indians attacked us.

Once I asked him why he carved on some trees during our hunt.

"I like to tell people I was there and maybe give them some news. I carved a beech tree near the Watauga River years back. It said 'I killed a bear.'" He smiled. "People still tell me they've seen it." I later learned other hunters in Kentucky and elsewhere liked to carve stuff on trees—their way of talking to each other.

Our winter trek ended without running into any Indians, and we came back to the fort in March with our sleds and horses piled high with dried meat, pelts, and skins. Colonel Boone would sell the pelts and skins, along with some of the meat.

As he told it, "When I was much younger, I used to take everything I got from hunting to Philadelphia. Those people there paid a darn good price. But then I spent the next few weeks having fun and frolicking, and spent all the money I'd earned."

Marrying Rebecca put an end to that."

Chapter 4

A Frightening Encounter

One hot Sunday in July, Jemima and I, along with Betsy and Frances Callaway, daughters of Colonel Callaway, decided to take a canoe and float on the Kentucky River. While all of us shared a ton of work from sunup to sundown—weeding the gardens, washing clothes, grinding corn, cooking and cleaning—there were times when we would have fun together, too. This promised to be one of them. The sun warmed our shoulders and backs as we drifted lazily in the sparkling river, and we dragged our arms through the water to cool ourselves. I couldn't remember when I'd been so relaxed.

Betsy used her paddle to guide the canoe, but the river current caught it and drew us toward the tree-lined shore a ways down on the other side of the river from the fort. For a while, we enjoyed the shade and the cool water. Suddenly, Jemima cried out, "Indians! There on the bank! Grab your paddles."

I looked up to see five Indians emerging from the trees no more than a few yards from our canoe. They'd been so silent, we'd hadn't seen or heard them until that moment. My heart raced as we grabbed our paddles in a panic and started to pull the canoe out into the river. But the Indians—a mixed group of Shawnee with their cloth head wraps and Cherokee wearing painted cloaks— waded in and grabbed the canoe before we could get underway. Jemima and I stood and used the paddles to strike the men holding onto the canoe, all of us screaming, hoping to alert someone on the other side of the river. Our attackers ignored being hit. Instead, they grabbed us about the waist, lifted us out of the canoe, and dragged us through the water to shore and into the trees. As the four of us stood together, dripping with water and shivering with fear, we could hear the Indians talking among themselves. Memories of the day my ma and pa died weakened me at the knees and I felt sick.

Jemima whispered, "I think they'll take us back to their tribe. Daddy told me these raiding parties kidnap women to add people to their tribes. I doubt they'll harm us. Most probably, they want us as slaves or wives."

Betsy asked," Do you think they'll ravish us?" Her pretty face twisted in fear. She was engaged to be married and probably thought if that happened, her betrothed wouldn't have her.

"No," replied Jemima, "at least not now. Maybe when we're with them long enough to become members of the tribe. Daddy told me they aren't violent with women captives, and they consider ravishing women during a raid to be a sin."

Looking at the knives and tomahawks in the Indians' belts, my stomach turned over again. "So you think our safest way to survive is to do what we're told? Can we leave a trail for anyone coming to rescue us?"

Jemima had learned much from her father. "We should bend branches, fall against bushes and break off twigs, grab berries as if to eat them, and leave some as we go along."

We all gasped as one of the Shawnees with a boldly painted face drew out his knife and held it at Jemima's throat, putting a finger to his mouth with his other hand. Clearly, we were not to speak. They prodded us into a line with their tomahawks, the Shawnee warrior with the painted face leading the group. Others walked on either side of us and a Cherokee brought up the rear. They pushed us to go fast,

24

heading north. We struggled to keep up, with our Sunday dresses catching on branches and roots, causing us to trip. My dress stuck to me with sweat and I bled where branches had cut me. But I realized that leaving some scraps of our dresses behind would increase our chances of being found.

Frances, also red-faced and out of breath, tugged on the Shawnee leader's cape, using her hands to try to tell him to slow down. But his stern blank face showed he didn't understand. So instead, we tripped and made ourselves fall, doing our best to slow the march. Jemima, who had a sore foot to begin with, fell the most, sprawling and screaming in pain, real or not. But still the Indians prodded and pulled us along. After a while, the only thing I could think of was keeping up the brutal pace.

By the time the sun dropped below the trees, the forest became too dim for us to see and we stumbled more and more. I think they must have figured out we could go no farther because when we finally came to a small clearing in the woods, they stopped and shoved us to the ground, where we leaned against each other for comfort. We looked at ourselves—our hair tangled with twigs and leaves, our faces dirty and streaked with sweat, and our dresses shredded. I couldn't remember when I'd been so hungry and thirsty, and I was too tired even to cry. They didn't light a fire and I wondered if they would give us any food or water.

When one of them came at us with a knife, we shrank back. But he only stooped down and chopped off the skirts of our dresses, up above our knees. Then he pulled off our ruined shoes and stockings.

"I need to pee," I whispered to Jemima. "How can I get them to understand that?"

Jemima stood, pointed at herself and us, gestured towards her private parts, and then started walking toward the trees. The Indians laughed, and one of them followed us, watching with no interest as we squatted to relieve ourselves on the forest floor. When we came back, they gave us water from a container made out of some sort of skin. It tasted terrible but none of us minded, only when the Indian holding the skin took it away.

We were forced to the ground again and tied together with braided rawhide rope. Shortly afterward, Jemima whispered she had a little penknife in her pocket, but none of us could reach it. The night air felt warm and, despite my fright, my eyes soon closed in sleep.

At dawn the next morning, our captors untied us and yanked us to our feet. We had become stiff overnight from the march the previous day, but once again we set off at a fast pace. We continued to break branches, strip leaves, and pull out vines, desperate to leave a trail. When the Shawnee leading us noticed this, he pulled out his knife and came at us. One of the Cherokee, who had a round, pleasant face and who had never shoved us, stood in front of him and said something I couldn't understand. The Shawnee backed off but began walking even faster. With neither rest nor any more water, we reached the point where we could not go on, and we sank to the ground one after another.

While we sat, panting, one of the Indians left to scout and came back with an old, sway-backed horse he'd found in the woods. They tried forcing us to ride it, maybe thinking if two of us rode, they could move faster. We could all ride, but we made like Jemima, who pretended she'd never seen a horse. Two Indians grabbed Betsy and me around the waist and easily flung us on top of the horse. Jemima and Frances pinched and kicked the poor animal, and when it bucked and tried to bite us, Betsy and I fell off. Our captors laughed at us, and with the laughter, they seemed to relax. Maybe they'd decided no one had followed them, because after we'd left the horse behind, we walked the next several miles more slowly, before stopping for the night.

No fire again, but at least we had water from a nearby stream. I drank until I thought I would burst. The Indians took something out of the pouches they wore on their belts and began to chew on it. Then they gave some to us. I tasted it—salted and dried buffalo tongue—and nearly gagged, but we were so hungry at that point that we all ate it.

That night, I found my tiredness overcame my feelings of fright and the fear of what lay ahead, but being tied up again, none of us slept well. Jemima thrashed and I could not stop rolling from one side to another, which caused Betsy to shush me and Frances to hiss at her. At first light, our captors yanked us up and prodded us to walk on. Midmorning, we forded a creek, where the four of us splashed ourselves with the cool water and drank as much as we could from our hands. "Delay them as long as you can," whispered Jemima, and we splashed some more and waded very slowly through the water, pretending to slip on the rocks.

The raiding party now followed something that looked like a buffalo trace, a path tamped down with many hoof prints and green scat here and there. To our amazement, they stopped to camp mid-afternoon. I figured I was right—the Indians felt that no one would rescue us at this point. Two left and came back after some time with meat from a buffalo calf and set it to roast over a fire. The smell of the roasting meat caused my stomach to rumble so loudly that one of the Shawnee laughed.

Although she wore a dirty wool cloak that the round-faced Cherokee had given her the previous night, Betsy shivered from her drying sweat. Wanting to warm herself, she approached the fire, where one of the Indians pulled on her hair, maybe in fun. Her face turned a dull pink and using a piece of bark near the fire, she scooped up some hot coals and dumped them on her tormentor's feet. When he hopped around in pain, the others laughed and one of them called her in English "a fine woman." Those words rekindled all my fear for our future.

Betsy then sat down on a log near the fire and began to cry. We gathered at her feet to comfort her. After some reassuring words from us, she stopped crying and soothed herself by picking through our hair, looking for lice—something we all did every day at the fort. I tried hard not to think horrible thoughts of being some Indian's woman. The hard, determined look on Jemima's face helped me to fight off my increasing despair.

Just then I heard a soft rustle somewhere up on the hill behind us, and Jemima twitched. Luckily, neither Frances nor Betsy heard it, nor did our captors. While one of the Indians tended the meat, two of the others gathered wood, another rested on the ground, and the fifth served as a lookout, concentrating on the path we'd taken. After a while, with all quiet except for the snap of fat from the roasting meat, the lookout leaned his gun against a tree and walked to the fire, pulling his pipe from his belt to light it. Jemima knew to keep still and gestured with her head. When I took a quick look where she'd indicated, I caught sight of Colonel Boone on the ridge above where we camped.

Suddenly we heard a shot from a long distance away, and the chest of the Indian at the fireside exploded in blood. The man fell into the fire but somehow got up and staggered into the forest. We all hit the ground, except for Betsy, who stood up, maybe to run. One of our captors picked up a piece of wood and swung at her head, but miraculously, the blow just grazed her. At that moment, Colonel Boone and his men charged down the slope from the ridge, whooping and hollering. The Indians fled, leaving behind their knives, tomahawks, and us.

Betsy, with her dark tangled hair, bare legs, and wool mantle, looked very much like an Indian, and one of the men turned his gun around, preparing to club her with its stock. I heard the colonel yell out, "Stop, you idiot! That's Betsy. We've traveled too far to save these girls. Now get down! We might be fired on."

Tense moments passed before Colonel Boone decided the Indians were not coming back. As I lay on the ground, the fear of the past days faded away, leaving me so limp I felt like I was melting into the dirt beneath me, but also filled with such happiness at our rescue. One of the men in the rescue party pulled me to my feet, and I joined the other girls. The men stood back in surprise when they got a good look at us.

"Jemima, you're a sight for sore eyes, but you're a real sight," said her pa.

He spoke the truth. Our clothes were in shreds, our dresses cut short, and blood and scabs decorated our skin, the result of scratches to our faces, arms and legs. We couldn't have been dirtier, and our eyes had become red and swollen from crying and lack of sleep. Samuel Henderson, Betsy's fiancé, wrapped her in his arms, whispering, "I'm so happy you're alive."

"Don't stand there staring at them! Get some blankets to cover them," Colonel Boone ordered, and we soon found ourselves wrapped warmly.

"Who fired that first shot?" the colonel asked. "I gave orders to hold your fire. You could have hit one of the girls." The man who'd fired first started to sob, but Colonel Boone put his hand on the man's shoulder, saying to him, "It's alright, nothing bad happened, thanks to God Almighty. The girls are safe." At that point, we girls sat back down and had a good cry.

The colonel decided not to go after the Indians. "I'll think we'll just head home in a while, after we've rested and eaten. I fear those Indians might be heading to join other raiding parties to the north and I'm not partial to following them."

Then we all ate well of the buffalo meat still roasting on the spit. I don't think I've ever tasted anything as good as that meat, before or since.

On the way back, we ran into the tired old horse the Indians had tried to make us ride. This time Fanny and Jemima got easily onto his back, while I felt strong enough to walk. At this point Betsy, who had soon become too tired to go on, fell to the ground. Sam asked her, "Can I offer you a ride?" When she looked puzzled, he turned his back and said, "Jump on." And that's how she returned to Boonesborough—on his back, with her hands clasped in front of Sam's neck and his arms holding her dangling legs.

A day later we reached the Kentucky River, where we sat and waited for the rescued canoe to ferry us across. I cannot describe the look on Mrs. Boone's face when she saw us coming up from the river. Hugging Jemima and me tightly, she laughed and cried. "I never thought to see you again."

The colonel, close behind, looked at his wife and said, "You don't have much faith in me, do you, woman?" But he smiled.

While our homecoming resulted in joyous reunions, our kidnapping was just the beginning of more warfare between the various Indian tribes and the settlers. Colonel Boone told us that during the time we'd been gone, a homestead just a half mile from

Boonesborough had burned to the ground, along with all the crops and an orchard of young apple trees. Settlers began to leave their outlying farms and crowd into Boonesborough and other forts for protection.

This news made me wonder how long it would be before the fort was attacked.

Chapter 5

Attack!

That fall, during one of his chats with the family after the evening meal, Colonel Boone told us that the colonists and the British were now fighting a war in the east. He called it the "war for independence" because the colonists wanted to be done with British rule and run the country themselves. Kentucky would hopefully be part of this new country.

He had more frightening news for us as well. "Rebecca, children, listen here. Indian raids are happening closer to us. The war parties are destroying crops and killing or stealing cattle and other farm animals. Boonesborough will likely be attacked but we don't know when. From now on, if you have to leave the fort, you have to go with some armed men." He squinted at Rebecca, as Thatch and me now called her. "You, too, wife. I know it's the season when you like to gather herbs and nuts and fruit and such in the forest, and I know you think you can take care of yourself, but me and Israel have to go with you."

Rebecca scowled.

I couldn't help but think of the attack on our farm and shivered at the thought of living through something like that again. *Would the walls of the fort and the men protect us?*

Thatch had become comfortable as part of the Boone family and when not distracted by chores, he took to following Colonel Boone around and occasionally getting in the way. He idolized him, and this new information energized his curiosity.

"Why are the Indians attacking the settlers?"

"It's pretty simple, Thatch," the colonel replied. "First of all, we've settled on Shawnee hunting grounds. The Shawnee want their land back, and the British have given them guns so they can drive us out. If the British gain control of these western territories, they can attack the those fighting for independence in the east from another front. The British and the Shawnee both think if they kill enough of us and starve the rest, we'll leave."

"Are we going to leave?" Thatch asked.

The thought of leaving didn't seem so terrible to me just now.

Colonel Boone gave us a grim smile. "No, this is *our* home now."

ଊ   ଌ

Over the winter, the people of Boonesborough became more relaxed, so when the first Indian attack on the fort occurred in March the next year, it came as a shock. We first heard gunfire coming from a grove of sycamore trees that grew nearby, and then the fort's sentry sounded a horn, so settlers who'd gone out to prepare for planting at their farms knew to return to the fort.

When I heard the shots and the horn, memories of what had happened to my ma and pa came rushing back and made me shake with terror. Rebecca hugged both me and Thatch, who'd wrapped his arms around my legs. She tried to calm us, saying, "We'll be all right. Daniel has our protection in hand. You go wait with the others in the cabin." Rebecca and Jemima then took their rifles and joined the men and a few other women guarding the fort. In the Boone home, tension became so thick I could almost taste it. The little ones fretted and cried, and Susannah, Levina and I did our best to soothe them.

The hours dragged on as we listened for more gunfire, but we heard none.

We waited inside for the rest of the day and everyone slept restlessly through the night, before Colonel Boone returned to the cabin to tell us the threat appeared to be over. "We fared pretty good. The Indians gave up, but not afore they killed a slave working in the field outside the fort and wounded the man who owned him. He'll recover. Rebecca's looking after him."

Jemima returned as well and helped Susannah, Levina and me prepare us a much-needed meal of cornbread and rabbit stew. While we ate, Colonel Boone told us, "I don't know what to think about the attack. Maybe this was just a warning? But we can't stop working the land if this place is to survive."

"But how can we do that?" I asked, while sitting with my back to the cabin wall, enjoying a full stomach and feeling a little less anxious. "The people in the fields will be wide open to ambush."

"I'm going to divide the men into two groups, one to guard and the other to farm. They can change out each day."

News reached us later that the Shawnee had attacked Harrodsburg the same day as us, with some deaths there. We all held our breaths as the men left the fort each day, but we suffered no more attacks for the rest of the month. Then at the end of April, on a day when the men who'd been scouting for signs of Indians returned and claimed they'd seen none, our cows gave us the first warning.

Thatch, who helped drive the cows to the pasture each day, came running back. "Colonel Boone, Colonel Boone. The cows won't go out! They're just hanging around the gate."

"Something's wrong, Thatch. Help bring them back inside. I'll send out two men to see what's happening."

When I overheard that, I resolved I would not go to look, but then curiosity overcame my fear and I went to the gate. Thatch had driven the cows back into the yard, and a few men stood at the gate, watching for the return of the two new scouts Colonel Boone had sent out. Among the men stood Simon Kenton. He often spent an evening talking quietly with the colonel, and the colonel had remarked several time what a fine marksman Kenton was. To my mind, his face seemed quite fierce, with large eyes, thick brows, a long nose and a large chin. But when he smiled, you had to smile back.

When we saw our scouts racing back to the fort, a small group of Shawnee came out of that darn Sycamore grove and fired at them. One of the men dropped, and an Indian jumped on his body, grabbing the man's hair and pulling out his knife. Thatch now stood beside me, watching, so I turned us away from seeing what I knew would happen.

Thatch struggled at first, telling me, "I want to see, I want to see," then pulled away just as my stomach roiled and I vomited into the dust.

Thatch stopped. "What's the matter, Eliza?"

I just shook my head, Thatch looking at me with concern. I wiped my mouth on my sleeve and when we both looked back at the scene happening outside the fort, we saw Mr. Kenton run from the fort, sight his rifle, and shoot the Shawnee waving the bloody scalp. "What's that he's holding?" asked Thatch.

"I'll tell you later."

"It's his scalp, isn't it? The girls told me that's what they do."

Poor Thatch. Our parents hadn't been scalped, but thinking about it turned my stomach again. I swallowed hard to keep down what remained of my last meal.

As we watched, the Indians scattered and Colonel Boone and Mr. Kenton, along with twelve others, pursued them. Trying to see, I decided to climb to the top of the palisade. Thatch, frustrated that he couldn't climb up, went back to peeking out from the gate. Just then Rebecca appeared behind me, carrying her rifle. As I started to climb, she pulled on my dress. "Eliza, stay down! You could be shot!"

"No, I don't think so. The Indians aren't even looking in the direction of the fort now." I was so driven to know if Colonel Boone would be okay, I shook off her hand and got to the top in time to see him and the other men surrounded by several dozen Shawnee. They'd emerged from the hollow where the sycamores stood, where they'd been waiting until our men came out to rescue the scouts. Now they blocked the men's way back. *Why hadn't Colonel Boone cut down those trees?* My hand went to my mouth and I stopped breathing. I couldn't bear to look, but I couldn't look away.

I heard Boone yell, "Boys, we have to fight." In reply, the men charged the Shawnee, swinging their guns and letting out a cry that chilled my blood.

By this time, Rebecca had climbed to the top of the palisade with her rifle, aiming it at the Shawnee. "They're too far away for a shot," she told me almost immediately, banging her hand in frustration on the palisade logs.

As we watched our men engaging the Indians at close quarters, I recalled Colonel Boone telling me that Indians disliked hand-to-hand fighting. But suddenly the colonel fell and he didn't rise. I heard a gasp from Rebecca when an Indian jumped on his body and raised his tomahawk. Seeing this, I shook so hard that I almost lost my hold and would have fallen if Rebecca hadn't grabbed me. Then a rifle fired, and the Indian fell to the ground, still holding the tomahawk. Mr. Kenton, who had been the last out of the fort, had gotten off that shot. When another Indian ran towards Colonel Boone, knife drawn, Mr. Kenton got between him and the colonel, swung the butt of his rifle, and crushed his head. Then he hoisted the colonel onto his shoulders and ran toward the fort, rifle balls spraying around him. I imagine the good Lord must have had a hand in saving them both, because all the shots smacked into the stockade wall on either side of them.

Another man, swinging his rifle, fought off the remaining Shawnee all by himself until everyone made it to the fort, then turned and ran, making it to safety without being hit. *Those Indians must be poor shots.*

Rebecca rushed to her husband and knelt beside him on the ground inside the gate, pulling off his bloody and ruined stocking. We could all see a rifle ball had smashed a good deal of bone in his ankle, which is why he'd fallen. "Carry him to our cabin, please," she asked, pointing at two of the men. "I'll tend to him and then I can take a look at the other wounded."

Thatch bounced around Colonel Boone as the men carried him, asking "Does it hurt? Are you going to be okay?" I knew he'd come to look on the colonel as his pa, and I could hear the anxiety in his voice. My own fear silenced me.

We had no doctors, but Rebecca had practice in removing bullets and treating wounds, and she physicked all the members of the family for various illnesses, cuts and rashes. Thatch and family members hovered as Rebecca removed the ball along with splinters of bone. While she concentrated on her doctoring, we heard the colonel grumble, "Damn, woman, can you not poke and pry so much?" This was accompanied by some loud groaning and the occasional unrepeatable word. When Rebecca had finished, she poured some liquor on the wound, producing a loud yelp from her husband, and then applied a poultice. Once her husband rested in bed, we all breathed a sigh of relief. Though we were happy he was alive, the possibility of infection remained a worry.

"Take these bloody rags and wash them," Rebecca said, handing them to me and Levina. "Boil them good."

શ્ર બ્ય

I sat in the cabin doorway the next day when Mr. Kenton answered Colonel Boone's request that he come visit. I knew the colonel wanted to thank him for saving his life and he seemed mighty flowery in his thanks, calling him "a brave man and a fine fellow."

"We both got lucky, Colonel Boone," Mr. Kenton replied.

The colonel was not a complainer by nature, but the next two months proved a trial for us all. Having to stay in bed with his leg heavily bandaged was almost as bad for his temper as the wound was for his ankle.

During May, Blackfish, the chief of the Shawnee, launched attacks on all the other forts in the area. This news caused me to be constantly on edge, despite Rebecca's best tries to distract me with work. It also irritated Colonel Boone no end—him still being laid up in bed—leading to some general cussing and yelling, which Rebecca bore with remarkable patience.

Then the Shawnee attacked Boonesborough again.

This siege lasted three days, which filled me with terror except for the few hours when I slept from exhaustion. The men took turns manning the palisade, and some women, too, wearing men's hats so it would look like we had more shooters. Only three men were wounded, but the biggest loss was the cattle still in the fields, butchered by the Shawnee warriors just before they decided to give up and leave. We recovered what meat we could from the poor animals, but everyone knew what this meant for our food supplies.

By this time, Colonel Boone could not be held down. He rose from his bed, saying, "Dammit, Israel, make me a crutch so I can get around. We need to improve the fort's defenses."

"I can do that," Israel replied, "but your ankle is not near healed. You're just going mess it up again." He made his pa a crutch, and the colonel surely tried his poor ankle getting around. As a result, he continued to have pain and a pronounced limp.

When another two hundred Shawnee attacked in July, hiding in the tall corn growing in front of the fort, the colonel sat in a chair near the gate and directed his men in defense of the fort. One man was killed and two others wounded, but we suffered another loss to our food supply when the Indians burned our corn before leaving. We watched it burn, smelling the roasting corn, knowing the Shawnee hoped to starve us out. By this time, I was so tired of being afraid, I didn't feel much of anything.

There were no more attacks that year, but those early ones meant we'd have a shortage of food that winter. In addition to the loss of the cattle, we harvested only a small amount of corn in the fall, with each family receiving just two bushels. The Indians seemed to be winning the war of starvation.

One cold morning, as I sat working in the cabin with the other girls, my stomach rumbled so loud I could hear it. I looked around, hoping no one else did, but this was now commonplace because we had so little food. I focused on salvaging the yarn from a sock too damaged to mend, winding the yarn in a ball, my fingers aching from the cold. Levina ground a little corn with a mortar and pestle, and Thatch and Jesse played with William, who was now toddling everywhere. Susannah stood outside, soaking nettle fibers in a large barrel of water to loosen them from their woody outer coating, and Jemima spun the loosened fibers with a drop spindle. Rebecca, always searching for new ways to make cloth, used a hand loom to weave the spun fibers together with buffalo hair. The resulting cloth was serviceable, although coarse, and very much needed, since we had no source of wool or flax and there was no way of obtaining store-bought goods.

A fire crackled in the hearth, and we'd wrapped ourselves in as much clothing as we owned, since the door had to stay open to let in light. My stomach growled again, and I asked Rebecca, "What are we going to do for food? We're all so hungry."

Rebecca looked up from her weaving. "I've been thinking on that. We'll have to depend on our hunting for meat. Since Colonel Boone's ankle is still doing poorly, he's offered room and board to a man by the name of William Cradlebaugh. He's an experienced hunter and will help provide us and the rest of the fort with meat."

"When will he get here?" asked the ever-curious Thatch. He tossed William in the air to a burst of giggles.

"Tomorrow, Thatch. I need you all to make him feel welcome. In the meantime, I want you girls to dig for turnips and potatoes in the fields—the Indians missed them—and then find the pawpaw trees along the edge of the forest. See if they have any fruit that hasn't been picked or maybe fell to the ground. Even if they're half eaten, dried up, or starting to rot, bring them in. We still have one milk cow and those chickens are laying, so I can make pawpaw pudding. But take Israel with you and bring your rifles."

There was a murmur of agreement to the idea of pawpaw pudding.

"Thatch," Rebecca continued, "after you gather eggs, I want you and Daniel Morgan to follow after the remaining cattle. Note what plants they eat. If they can eat them, so can we. After Israel and you girls get back and Thatch and Daniel Morgan have brought us some of those greens, you all take your rifles and go look for nuts. Our supply is low, especially the acorns."

I had hunted for nuts earlier that month with Levina and Jemima, and we'd returned with a bag full of walnuts, hickory nuts and hazelnuts. But she sent us back out to gather acorns, which could be ground into flour. I'd learned they had to be dried, ground, and the flour leached in water for about two weeks to get rid of the bitterness. The flour made good flat cakes, mixed with a little cornmeal. We always had acorns somewhere in this process.

Cradlebaugh proved a grand addition to our large family. A few years earlier, a hunting party had driven some wild hogs into the woods nearby. Those hogs still foraged there and had produced lots of piglets every year. I'd heard the adults were so ferocious, even wolves wouldn't attack them. But Colonel Boone had Cradlebaugh hunt those hogs for their meat, and he did a good job providing it, most of which we salted and stored.

One day in early January, after another meager meal of squirrel meat, boiled greens, and corn mush flavored with hog fat, the colonel announced, "I'm heading up to the salt licks on the Licking River sometime soon. These here greens and mush aren't too tasty without any salt, and we've about run out of it. Pretty soon we won't have enough left to preserve meat from the game we kill."

Rebecca frowned. "That's a great risk, Daniel."

"I think it's a risk we need to take."

"Those salt licks are really far away, Daddy," Jemima said, worry creasing her forehead.

"Far enough, near thirty miles."

"Can I go?" Thatch jiggled with the excitement of a trek.

"No!" Colonel Boone surprised us by yelling. "This is no trip for young 'uns. There's too much danger from the Shawnee. Boiling salt is a man's work, Thatch, which is why I'm taking a lot of men with me. We're leaving in two days, once we've got together everything we need."

Over the next two days, I helped Rebecca pack food and supplies for the trip. I knew we had to have salt to preserve meat, but I didn't understand how you could get salt from a river. So I asked her how that could be.

"Well, Eliza, in this part of the country, salt is often found in springs. We call them salt licks. We boil water from the salt licks in large kettles over fires dug into the ground. After the water boils away, the salt is left. But it takes a lot of water to get the salt. This will be a long and hard job for those men. And dangerous."

"How long do you think they'll be gone?"

"Maybe two months or more, all told..."

"Why are the men are going to the salt licks right now?" I asked. "It's January and darned cold."

Rebecca gave her low-throated, soft laugh. "Daniel thinks they'll be safer from Indian attacks this time of year. He knows that area real well and figures he can scout for Indians, hunt to supply the men with meat and run traps, while the rest of the men boil the water."

"So we won't see any of the men again until they've collected all the salt we need?"

"No, some of them will return with packhorses carrying the salt they've harvested, and then others will go back to the licks with supplies needed by the men collecting the salt."

⁐ ⁐

Colonel Boone, as well provisioned as Rebecca could manage, left with about thirty men in the coldest part of January. They took pack horses carrying flour, salted meat, potatoes and other food, blankets, pots for cooking, and large iron cauldrons for boiling the water.

As the days passed and we heard nothing, our fear and frustration grew. Finally, after a month, some of the men came back with a few hundred bushels of salt, and another crew left with supplies to relieve the rest of the first group. In the colonel's absence, we hunted together to provide for the family, as well as doing the absent men's chores, like splitting wood. We missed the colonel's presence sorely, but Rebecca kept us very busy.

In April, Flanders Calloway and Thomas Brooks, two men from the salt-seeking party showed up at the fort, along with some of the men who'd been sent out with supplies. Everyone came running for news. These men told us they'd been out hunting when a large number of Shawnee had appeared at the salt licks camp. After asking for water, Simon Kenton, who had saved Colonel Boone's life in the first attack on the fort, said, "The Shawnee's chief, Blackfish, captured Colonel Boone while he hunted for meat for our party." The news shocked everyone into silence but affected Rebecca most of all. She sat right down on the ground, her face crumpled, as she fought to hold back tears.

The next news hit us even harder. "Because they were greatly outnumbered," Kenton told us, "Colonel Boone apparently persuaded the men to surrender, rather than fight and most certainly die."

"Then why aren't you among the captured?" Flanders' pa, Richard, asked.

"On the day of the capture, Pa, Colonel Boone hunted to the south, while me and Thomas hunted north. We got lucky and the Shawnee never saw us. It was snowing hard, and when we got back to the camp, we saw most of the salt scattered in the snow and mud on the river banks, and many foot and horse prints leading north. All our supplies and equipment, including the kettles were gone, but we figured since there were no bodies, Colonel Boone had done a fine dance convincing Blackfish to take the men as slaves. We found these others hiding in the woods.

"Have you any news of those that were taken?" Rebecca asked, having been helped to her feet.

Kenton replied, "I tracked them for a while, long enough to know they continued on north towards Ohio."

I stood close to Rebecca's side, listening to all this. "Do you know what will happen to them?" she asked Kenton in a flat voice.

"I do not," he replied.

"So they might kill him or sell him as a slave?'

Kenton just shook his head.

☙ ☙

Days turned into weeks, and still we heard nothing more of Colonel Boone and the men. I knew Rebecca tried not to think that that the men taken had been killed, but she knew what happened to those captured by Indians. She hardly spoke to us except for giving out the chores. Without her normal strength, we found it hard to keep our spirits up. She roamed restlessly at night, and I often woke to see her standing in the cabin doorway, a blanket around her shoulders.

Then grumbling started in the fort, and I overheard one man say, "Boone's not returned. And you know he would've tried to escape. I bet he's gone over to the British."

"Maybe he's been killed," another said.

"Nah, he's surrendered. We're on our own."

As the days passed with still no sight of the colonel or any of the men, mutterings about him being a turncoat grew — until most of the fort's residents, with the exception of the Boone family, believed it to be true. I figured this came from fear of another raid by Blackfish and the Shawnee without Colonel Boone there to lead them, but eventually even Rebecca seemed to think he might not come back.

Chapter 6

A Shock for Us All

As the days turned into months without word of Colonel Boone, and with the ever-present threat of a raid by Blackfish leading the British and the Shawnee, the rumblings about his defection grew louder, and the other settlers glared at our family as if we were to blame.

Various officers of the Virginia militia wanted to take command of the fort, and without the colonel around to lead us, the rivalries between these officers made the situation inside the fort even worse—with no one in charge of anything, nothing got done. Conditions deteriorated. Dead animals, filth swept from the cabins, pig excrement, and the odor of so many people living in close quarters made some sick. No one wanted to go outside the fort to hunt, farm, or look for food. Occasionally one of the Boones and I would slip out to hunt through the largely unguarded back gate, and we all worked to keep the cabin and ourselves clean. It helped that the river ran just behind the fort so we could bring in water. Rebecca did her best to feed us, but we had no bread, fruits, or vegetables. Just meat.

By spring, the long months of waiting and hoping took its final toll. After another poor evening meal of salted pork and acorn flat cakes, Rebecca stood up and told us she thought the fort had become unlivable. "I'm supposing that your pa is dead," she stated in a flat and emotionless voice. "Today I ran into Mr. Bryan, who just came back from spending the winter with his family in Carolina. He told me he'd ran into some Kentuckians in Moccasin Gap. They told him everyone in the salt-making party had been murdered by the Shawnee." Her voice broke and her eyes filled with tears. Jemima got up and put an arm around her mother, who looked down at the floor for a moment or two. Finally she raised her head. "I've decided to leave our troubles here in Kentucky and travel to our family in Yadkin. I'm taking you all with me."

My heart sank with her words. Everyone tried to talk at once until Jemima shushed us, saying to her mother, "Flanders and me thought you would decide to leave. But I don't think Daddy's dead, Mama. I'm not giving up hope. We're going to stay here." Her voice wavered because she hardly ever argued with her strong-willed mother.

While the rest of us held our breaths, Rebecca's face got hard, sort of like stone. She squinted at Jemima. "You're just as pig-headed as your pa. Stay if you like, but I'm leaving with everyone else in two days."

Hearing this tore me in two. Thatch and I owed so much to Colonel Boone and also to Rebecca. But in my heart, I just knew he lived and that certainty told me what I had to do. After a moment, I stood up next to Jemima. "I'm staying, too," I said in a shaky voice.

Rebecca shook her head. "That's your choice, Eliza. I wish you'd come with us, but you're old enough now to take your own path."

I looked over at Thatch. I knew he would yell out he wanted to stay with me, but I cut him off. "Thatch, you go with Rebecca. You're just too young to stay here. It's very important to me that you're safe, and Ma and Pa would want this, too."

He slumped down with his arms folded, the picture of rebellion. "I want to stay, Eliza."

"I know that, son," replied Rebecca, "but your sister's right. You need to come with us."

Thatch broke into tears and ran out of the cabin. I let him go.

⊱　⊰

On the first day of May, on a bright, sun-lit morning, Thatch, Rebecca and the rest of the Boone family left for Yadkin. They would travel on foot, with a small supply of meat for food and the clothes on their backs, in the company of some soldiers who were abandoning Kentucky.

The colonel's cat wrapped itself around my legs as I hugged Thatch and told him to be brave and mind what Rebecca told him. Both of us cried. Jemima and I hugged Rebecca in turn, Jemima's eyes filling with tears.

"Travel safe, Mama, and send us a letter when you reach Yadkin."

Rebecca stepped back and took her daughter by her shoulders. "You take care of yourself. I hope Daniel does return, even though it seems like I've given up hope. Tell him I waited as long as I could."

I put an arm around Jemima's waist to comfort her and myself as well, as we watched them leave. Thatch turned to wave before they disappeared down the trail, but I could hardly see him because of my tears.

Word reached us shortly after Rebecca left that Andrew Johnson, one of the men taken at Salt Licks, had escaped from the Shawnee encampment at Chillicothe and had made his way to Harrodsburg. The frontier news line reported what he'd said when asked about Colonel Boone: Boone was a Tory, had surrendered all of them up to the British, and took an oath of allegiance to the British.

Johnson's words increased the feelings among many living here that the colonel was a traitor.

ⅎ ⅋

At the end of June, God answered our prayers. Colonel Boone appeared by the river one morning. He'd escaped from Blackfish!

Jemima and I came running with full hearts when we heard the news, only to find a man who didn't look much like her pa. So thin we could count his ribs, he'd had his hair plucked out by the Indians, leaving just a top knot, and he wore only some raggedy short pants. Jemima and I were so shocked we couldn't even speak.

His eyes scanned the faces of the crowd surrounding him, stopping when he came to us. "Jemima. Eliza," he said quietly.

Jemima and I went up to her pa and hugged him, tears running down our cheeks. After a few moments, he pulled away and looked around again. "Where's Rebecca and the rest of the family?"

"She left over a month ago, Daddy. After so long, she thought you were dead. I think she just ran out of hope, so she took the family back to Yadkin."

His knees buckled then, and with the support of Flanders, Jemima's husband, and Simon Kenton, he walked slowly to the cabin, which stood mostly empty. They half-carried him inside, where he sat wearily sat on the bench by the table. Jemima and I had followed them inside and took a place on either side of her pa. Flanders sat near the hearth, stunned by the colonel's sudden return. "I'll see you later, Colonel Boone," said Mr. Kenton, before leaving. "You rest up."

"Oh, Daddy," said Jemima, leaning into him. "We truly thought you were dead. Mr. Bryan told us some settlers had said so. Eliza and

I just couldn't believe that, so we stayed." Her eyes filled with tears again and she got up and put her arms around him from behind. "I'm so happy to see you," she sobbed. "What happened to you?"

The colonel gave us a weak smile and said, "That's a long story. First I want to know why no one was pleased to see me. They seemed afraid of me."

"I'm so sorry to tell you this, colonel," I said, "but news reached us that Andrew Johnson had reached Harrodsburg after escaping from Blackfish's camp. He told the people there that you'd arranged for the surrender of the salt boilers and had become a son of Blackfish. He also said you were happy as a pig in mud to be living with the Shawnee. And he mentioned you'd taken a wife and had promised to surrender Boonesborough to Blackfish in the spring. Rebecca and your family and I never believed that, but Richard Calloway and some others accepted this load of hogwash because you'd been away so long. They truly think you've gone over to the British."

Colonel Boone slammed his fist on the table. "Johnson—that low down pile of buffalo dung don't know anything. He was one of the most experienced woodsmen in that group at Salt Licks, but he played the fool for the Indians, pretending to be all mental and confused after being captured. And dang if the Shawnee didn't believe him, since they think anyone with madness is blessed. They even gave him a name—Pecula or Little Duck. When he ran away, they were mighty concerned for his safety, thinking he couldn't survive in the wilderness."

Flanders spoke to his pa-in-law from where he sat by the hearth. "You need to know that Johnson's words made these men think you sold out Boonesborough and possibly all the Kentucky settlements to the British. They think you're just waiting for the British and the Shawnee to arrive. Watch your back here in the fort."

Colonel Boone grunted and said with a sigh, "After all this time, it seems they just don't know me." At that point, the cat jumped up in his lap, and he smiled for the first time as he stroked her.

We knew everyone wanted to hear what he had to say, and some men and women had gathered outside our cabin. Jemima went out and told them, "Come back tomorrow after he's had some sleep." Then she shut the cabin door.

It took a bit for me to recover from the shock of seeing him in such rough condition, a man everyone had thought dead come back to life. I had no idea what he would tell us, but as I sat beside him, my heart jumped for joy that he'd come home.

After resting for a bit, Colonel Boone bathed in the river, and Jemima found some clothes for him, thinking he would be more acceptable to the people of the fort if he looked more settler than Shawnee. She complained miserably that she could do nothing about his hair, but she did cut off the top knot.

Jemima and I had made a stew from rabbit meat and a few early vegetables from the garden, which she served to her pa, Flanders and me. The cat, having had little to eat but mice since Rebecca left, lurked under the table, waiting for the scraps she knew she'd get from the colonel.

In between mouthfuls, with weariness dripping from his voice, Colonel Boone said, "I've come, mostly running, about 160 miles in the last four days. I ate only once in all that time, the hump from a buffalo I killed near Blue Licks, so you'll excuse my eagerness for food." He quickly emptied his bowl. "This tastes mighty fine, Jemima. Don't mind if I have more." While Jemima went to fill his bowl again, he leaned down and gave a bit of meat to the cat.

Jemima returned with his bowl, saying, "After this, Daddy, you should get some sleep. I've got you a blanket that Mama left behind. Time enough to tell us more after you've rested."

‗ ‗

The next morning, after a long and deep sleep, the colonel sat down on a stump outside the cabin to speak to us and others who'd gathered there. Many more had come, interested in finding out about his time with the Shawnees and about his escape.

"Well, I'll begin with what happened to the salt party, folks. Some Shawnee spotted me when I was out hunting. Since I'd loaded my horse with deer meat, he couldn't run, so I jumped off him and ran myself. I'd run maybe a mile when they started firing at me. At that point, I figured I weren't young enough to outrun them, so I leaned my gun against a tree trunk and surrendered. They took me to where Blackfish and over a hundred Indians, painted for war, had gathered. Two French Canadian traders and a man I knew, Will Emery, had joined them."

"How did you know this man, Colonel?" I asked. "He's not from around here."

"No, indeedy, he took me prisoner eight years ago when he discovered me exploring on the Kentucky River. He's called a yellow jacket—a man who's been working with the British and the Indians. But this time he shook my hand and smiled. When I explained I was in command of Boonesborough, danged if a bunch of them Indians didn't come forward to shake hands with me. Mighty strange."

Mr. Cradlebaugh moved in closer to Mr. Boone. "We heard when you met with Chief Blackfish, you persuaded him not to attack us," he said.

"Yup. Blackfish had organized this raiding party and planned his next stop to be Boonesborough. He told me he knew it weren't defended very well. I did a lot of palavering to convince him that any women and children he captured wouldn't survive a winter trek back to Detroit. But I had to promise Blackfish I'd go with him to Boonesborough in the spring and get the people here to surrender.

"But Blackfish wanted more. He wasn't happy waiting to attack the fort. So I had to dicker. I told him I could get the men making salt to surrender and that they would most probably survive the march to Ohio country. Then he could adopt them into his tribe or the British would pay a ransom for them."

"How did you talk the men into surrendering, Daddy?" asked Jemima.

"Well, when they took me back to the salt licks, I found the men there had been surrounded by more Shawnee, and I told them they'd all be massacred if they didn't surrender. Which was true. Many of them Indians wanted to kill us all in revenge for us killing one of their chiefs a while back."

I shivered at his words. If Colonel Boone hadn't been successful in his haggling with Blackfish, maybe they would have gone ahead with the plan to attack Boonesborough and we would have been killed, too. I wondered if these back-and-forth killings would ever end. Jemima, probably thinking the same thing, just stared at her pa.

"So did Blackfish end up saving you?" asked Flanders, who sat on the ground not far from where the colonel perched on his stump.

"No, son, but he called a council of all the Shawnee present to decide our future. I spoke to them in English, and someone translated. I felt more nervous than a treed raccoon, but I kept talking and talking. Maybe they got tired of listening to me or maybe I did a good job convincing them, because they voted to let us live, fifty-one to forty-nine. A close one, by God.

"We left the next morning for Chillicothe. At the end of the first day, they made me run a gauntlet of their warriors."

"What's a gauntlet, Colonel?" I asked.

"Well, Eliza, it's a kind of torture and punishment for their prisoners. You have to run between two lines of Indians who can strike you as hard as they can with anything at hand. I got lucky. Most of them hit me lightly, but some wanted to kill me. I made it to the end, but not without some of them landing hard blows that sent me staggering out of the gauntlet. And I bled like a stuck pig from a cut on the top of my head." He leaned down to show the scar. "I leveled the last Indian in the gauntlet by using my head to knock him down flat. After that, the Indians shook my hand again and called the one who'd I'd knocked down a woman.

"The Shawnee made us to trek a hundred miles in the snow to the Little Miami River, carrying some of the salt, kettles and other equipment on our backs. Then we turned west to go to Chillicothe, getting to their village there around the end of February—it's way north, in the place called Ohio. We had to run another damn gauntlet when we got there. I guess the new group of Shawnee wanted to their turn to punish us. But we were lucky, we all survived. Well, one man got his arm broke."

At this point, Jemima intervened because her father wavered and looked like he would fall off the stump. He was thin as a rail and his face, with his bones clear under his skin, looked sort of gray.

She faced the crowd and said, "Folks, can you give my father some time to rest again before he answers more of your questions? He'll talk to you again tomorrow."

I could hear grumblings, but Colonel Boone had the last word. "I only just bought us some time. Blackfish's coming here and soon. We got to repair the fort before he gets here."

The crowd's buzzing changed in tone, and Jemima led our way into the cabin.

Chapter 7

We Prepare for an Attack

The next morning, the colonel resumed his seat on the stump. Flanders had moved it somewhat farther out in the yard because the growing interest in his tale had drawn yet more people. "Now where was I?' he asked, more to himself than us.

"You had to run another gauntlet at Chillicothe," a voice yelled from the back of the crowd.

"Right. Well, after our introduction to the tribe, the Shawnee adopted all but ten of us. I know that sounds strange, but they liked us. They thought we were strong and brave, even dignified, and they needed to replace family members who'd been killed in raids. That's their way. Chief Blackfish decided to adopt me as a son to replace a son who'd been killed.

"And it ain't all that pleasant to be adopted. The old women scrubbed me in river water cold enough to freeze my..." and here he stopped himself for a moment, causing some of the men to snicker. "They did that to get out all my white blood, then they plucked out my hair, except for that tuft at the top. More painful than running the gauntlet, I swear." He passed his hand over the top of his head, where his hair was just growing in around what little Jemima had left of that tuft. "Afterward, I went to the council house where Blackfish speechified about my adoption and gave me my new name—Sheltowee. It means big turtle."

That got some hoots.

"With that name, I became part of the tribe. They even took me to Detroit, along with the ten prisoners Blackfish wanted to trade for money. The governor at Detroit, Henry Hamilton, offered them a hundred pounds in silver for me, but Blackfish refused."

"Is that when you turned to the British side?" another man asked.

I don't think I'd ever seen Colonel Boone get so mad. His face froze up and he flushed a deep red. He stood up. "Whoever believes that doesn't know me and calls me a coward. I've never been disloyal! I just wanted to escape and come home, so I decided in order to do that, I'd be friendly with all of them, maybe catch them off guard at some point. Which I did. Could any of you done better?"

The undercurrent of grumbling in the group of listeners dropped to a bare whisper. What the colonel had said rung true, because everyone knew him as a great palaverer, a man who could talk himself out of anything.

He sat back down on the stump. "Blackfish always had a couple a Shawnee shadowing me, so I didn't have much chance to run off. But then Blackfish brought me along when he led a party to the salt licks on the Scioto River. I overheard him persuading a new group of Shawnee, who had joined him there, to help him take Boonesborough the next month, so I knew I had to get out of there. On the way back from the salt licks, the Shawnee spotted some turkeys in the trees and ran off to kill some. I cut the straps on my horse to dump the salt it was carrying and galloped off with just a blanket tied to my back, old pants, a rifle that had no stock and one bullet.

"I ran that horse until it collapsed, then continued on foot. When I got to the Ohio River, I made a raft to cross it and kept going. I used a fallen sourwood sapling to make a stock for the rifle and tied the stock to the rifle with hide strings from the blanket. That rifle was good enough to shoot a buffalo. After three days with no food, that buffalo hump tasted mighty good. That meal lasted me long enough to get here."

I thought the people listening would realize he'd traveled 160 miles in under four days and that what he'd gone through would have killed any other man. It should have been enough to shut their mouths, but it wasn't.

After he finished his telling, Colonel Boone met with the leading men of Boonesborough to persuade them to repair and strengthen the fort. His reasoning and smooth talking served him well, but of course, they put him in charge of the work. Most of the people in the fort agreed to help prepare Boonesborough for what was certainly coming, and I think the fear of a possible attack lessened the questions about the colonel's loyalty, at least for a time. I had no idea how much work was needed, but with everyone imagining what would happen if the Shawnee took the fort, whatever he asked to be done… got done.

When he asked the women to pool their food stores so everyone living within the fort could be fed, they grumbled at his request but did see the sense of it. All the extra food they gathered got stored at Boone's smithy, which stood in the middle of the fort ground. Then Jemima and I helped the women make a load of bandages from ragged clothes.

Colonel Boone's brother, Squire Boon, lived with his family in the fort and had been a great source of support to the colonel over the years. He'd accompanied his brother when he blazed the Wilderness Trail through the Cumberland Gap, and Squire's family had been among the first to settle here. An expert blacksmith, he'd taught Jemima how to mold bullets. It seemed I would learn, too, after the colonel told me it would make me more useful.

One morning, I watched as Jemima built up a very hot fire in the smithy. "Luckily almost everyone's rifle is a flintlock, otherwise we'd have to make different bullets for each gun. That would be some job." She pointed to some scissor-like metal things beside the fire. "See the molds there? They're called scissor molds. If you squeeze the handles, the mold for the ball opens up."

I tried it. "So how do you get the lead into the mold?" By this time, both of us were sweating pretty well from the heat, and I pushed some strands of damp hair out of my face.

"If you let the handles go, the mold comes together. Look closely, and you'll see a small hole on the top. You pour the lead through there, then you let the mold cool. After the lead gets solid, you squeeze the handles to release the ball and then file off its rough edges."

"Sounds like a slow process."

She smiled, "Yup. That's why there's a bunch of these molds and you're here to help me. Good thing the lead cools fairly quickly. Squire is working on a mold that will hold four balls. For now, just be careful not to burn yourself handling the melted lead and the hot balls. There's some leather gloves over there we can wear." She placed a long-handled pot containing lead scraps over the fire. "Time to start. Hopefully, some others will come along to help us."

ഔ   ഌ

To keep our spirits up, some of the men and women had planted corn in the fields outside the fort, with squash at the base of each stalk and beans to climb the corn, in the Indian way. Cucumber and pumpkins grew alongside. They'd also planted vegetable gardens with turnips, lettuce, peas, potatoes, carrots and onions. The sight of the growing vegetables lifted our hearts and once harvested, made a welcome addition to our table.

A beehive of activity hummed inside the fort. While we slowly stocked the fort's magazine with lead balls, the noise of building filled the air—sawing, pounding, grunting, the yelling of orders. The huge logs making the fort walls had to be repaired or replaced. The fourth side of the fort had to be finished, and the blockhouses at each corner completed. Some men tackled digging a well, since up until now we had lugged water from the river behind the fort. Both Mr. Callaway, one of Mr. Boone's most vocal critics, and Colonel Boone himself sent letters asking for reinforcements from the Virginia militia, since we'd be outnumbered by Blackfish's army.

As the summer dragged on, the already hot air in the fort grew hotter with tension, long hours of back-breaking work, short tempers and the occasional fight. All of us worked off and on at harvesting, a relief from the tense mood.

Jemima and I foraged for berries and fruit in the woods, taking our rifles and accompanied by her husband or Israel Boone.

One very hot day, Jemima, Flanders and I set out to see if we could find some ripe elderberries, mulberries or serviceberries in the woods. I thought I'd spotted a plum tree on a previous trip out and also hoped to find some paw-paws, so I wandered off in that direction without saying anything to Jemima and Flanders. They didn't notice, and I knew they'd be grateful for some time alone.

I felt lucky when I found both ripe plums and paw-paws and filled my sack to the top with the fruit. By the time I finished picking, the sweat dripped down my neck and back, and I followed the splashing sound of running water to a small brook, where I took off my moccasins and waded in, slopping water up my arms. Finally, I just sat down in it and enjoyed its coolness, breathing in the warm smell of vegetation and watching the leaves in the trees move with a light breeze. I had just tilted my head back to catch the sun when I heard quiet steps farther along the brook's edge. When I turned to find the source of the noise, a Shawnee appeared. I stood up quickly, water running from my clothes. We stared at each other.

I guessed his age at no more than twelve or thirteen, his face still rounded. He wore a breach clout and leggings, and red stripes painted his face and chest. Eagle feathers stuck out from his topknot. I supposed coming upon a young, white woman alone in the woods, clothed in a ragged dress with its hem pulled through a belt to make pants, surprised him. He stopped short. When he started to come toward me, I put my finger up to my lips and then held up two fingers, pointing them in the direction where I'd last seen Jemima and Flanders. I thought if he knew I was not alone, he might not take me.

He hesitated, and I wondered if I could give him something to distract him. I reached up and pulled out the ribbon that bound up my hair. *Red and frayed, but maybe he'd like it.* I held it out and nodded. Just then, we both heard the sound of voices. The Shawnee boy grabbed the ribbon and ran, and I sank to my knees in the brook, shivering with relief.

Flanders and Jemima appeared, smiling, then puzzled by my appearance—kneeling in the brook, hair about my shoulders, and probably as pale as the underside of a rock. "What's the matter, Eliza?" Jemima asked, taking off her moccasins and sitting down with her feet in the water. "Is the water too cold?"

"A Sh-sh-shawnee. Just here," I stammered out.

"Which way did he go?" Flanders asked me, looking around for any movement.

"Too late to follow him. But he could be part of a larger party."

Jemima immediately stood up, slipped into her moccasins and pulled me to my feet. "We need to go. Now!"

ॐ   ॐ

The boy may have been on his own, since no attack occurred that day or later in the week. In the meantime, Mr. Hancock, a former prisoner of the Shawnee who'd been taken in the capture of the salt-boilers, appeared in the woods on the other side of the river. I left the smithy when I heard people yelling and went to see him, along with probably half the fort's population. He'd arrived naked and exhausted, but after getting some clothes to cover himself and eating some smoked meat, he asked to speak to Colonel Boone. Because of his weakness, men had to carry him to the colonel, who at the time struggled along with several others to set a huge log in a hole for the palisade. Of course, I, along with a crowd of curious people, followed Hancock.

The colonel was so intent on setting the log that he didn't realize who'd come to see him, until Mr. Hancock called out, "Colonel Boone, I am returned."

The colonel looked up, his face lifting in surprise. "Will, is that you? Ain't you a sight for sore eyes!" He clapped Hancock on the shoulder. "You look done in—sit yourself down. He motioned to an upended stump, where the men carrying Hancock sat him down. Colonel Boone dropped to the ground beside him. "Tell me how you escaped. And what news of Blackfish?"

Hancock moved on the stump, groaning a little. "Captain Will – you remember that Shawnee? – adopted me." His bald head and top knot confirmed this statement. "Somehow he got the notion I'd try to escape and warn you, after you'd run off. Blackfish knew from his spies that you'd made it back here and had started strengthening the fort. So Captain Will made me take my clothes off every night, and he slept in front of the door, just to keep me from escaping. But when he got himself drunk at a nighttime war council, I snuck out, with no clothes and nothing but some dried corn. Got lost after I crossed the Ohio and figured I'd just as soon die, but I found a tree where I'd carved my name on a hunt. That's how I knew which way to go."

"Well, we're right glad to see you. Do you know when Blackfish will attack?" That question was met by dead quiet as everyone strained to hear his answer.

"Blackfish is still waiting. He wants British and French soldiers to march with them, along with another four hundred Indians I heard were coming. I'm betting it'll be soon."

Groans came from the onlookers.

Boone thought for a minute, then asked, "Will, could you do right by me and tell these good people here I saved the salt boilers' hides last winter? They seem to think I'm a traitor."

"You ain't no traitor, Colonel Boone. But I'm puzzled why you'd seemed cheerful at Chillicothe and content to live with them dirty Shawnee. That did make me sorta mad, along with some of the other men."

"Well, that was how I decided to gain their trust. I did my dang best to let them think I enjoyed living with them, and it seems I succeeded if you thought that. Thataway, they came to trust me and when the time came, gave me a chance to escape."

"Well, you did do that," Hancock admitted.

With that, the conversation ended, and Jemima, who'd joined me, hoped the suspicions about the colonel's loyalty had been put to rest. Unfortunately, we heard Hancock mutter as he walked away, "I still heard Boone promise to give up the fort to the Indians and said he'd give them everything."

Chapter 8

Chief Blackfish Makes His Move

Under Colonel Boone's direction, the men completed strengthening of the fort by summer's end. Everyone had harvested their corn by then, and I felt safer than I had in a long time with our loft full of dried corn and corn meal, preserved meat, and vegetables and nuts we'd gathered from our gardens and the woods. We also had an overflowing supply of general provisions stored at the smithy.

We waited and waited. But for some reason the Shawnee attack that Mr. Hancock and the colonel had warned about didn't happen. The fear we'd all felt earlier, which had driven our hard work, began to lessen. It seemed Hancock's report might be true—that Blackfish would postpone the raid until he could gather a larger force. However, our expected reinforcements from the Virginia militia didn't arrive.

Some of the men, exhausted from their labors reinforcing the fort and feeling less fear of an attack, became restless. Colonel Boone appeared anxious to do something, anything. All the settlers gathered at the meeting where he proposed a scouting expedition across the Ohio River.

"I think we should raid the Shawnee in their own homes," he said, "just to let Blackfish know we're not sitting back but are ready and willing to fight. We could use this as a scouting trip to find out just where the Shawnee are now."

Richard Calloway immediately objected. "This is stupidity, Boone. You're going to weaken the defenses here at Boonesborough, just when the Shawnee might attack. I'll not go along with this!"

The colonel replied, "I know a village on Paint Creek, not far on the other side of the Ohio River, where the Indians are rich in good horses and beaver fur. We could go, have a great carouse, and get back in time to face Blackfish."

"This is madness," Calloway yelled, red in the face.

Jemima and I tended to side with Calloway, her pa-in-law, in thinking this plan was foolish. Despite the objections, the colonel soon left with about thirty eager men.

Later that day, while grinding corn with Jemima, I asked, "Why do you think your pa decided to leave the fort for a raid? I'm more anxious now than I've been in weeks that we'll be attacked and not able to defend ourselves."

After a moment, she replied, "Me, too. I worry Flanders will be killed if they raid any Shawnee villages. But Daddy can be pigheaded, and all those people saying he's disloyal hurt him sorely. Maybe he figured it would quiet them down if he showed some military leadership."

I nodded. "And those men that went with him were itching for an adventure, after all their hard work this summer. Maybe bringing back horses and furs will be good for them."

"I know Daddy was dead set on showing Blackfish that Shawnee villages could be raided, too, maybe to make him think again about raiding *us*." Jemima sounded like her pa.

ℝ ℞

Colonel Boone and the men returned in less than a week, empty-handed and worn down.

"What happened?" Jemima asked Flanders, as soon as he and her father entered the cabin.

Flanders shook his head and sat down at the table, where cornbread and a stew made with pork fat, potatoes and carrots had been set out for them. "We put together some rafts so we could cross the Ohio River. But who'd we run into as soon as we landed? A band of Shawnee, that's what, probably on their way to join Blackfish."

"What did you do?" I sat down at the table with them and helped myself to some bread. I always seemed hungry. Maybe because I kept growing out of my clothes.

Colonel Boone answered. "Well, we had a mite of a skirmish. Killed two, wounded one, then hightailed it out of there as fast as we could. Almost collided with a larger group of Shawnee south of the Ohio, along with a company of British militia. We circled around them because they stood between us and here. With Blackfish camped close by here at the Blue Licks, I figure they'll be here tomorrow." He dug into the stew and sopped up the remains with bread. "Mighty good, whichever of you made this."

Jemima beamed.

"Did everyone make it back?" I asked.

"We left two behind to spy on the Shawnee," he replied, running his hand over the longer growth of hair now on his head. "Anything happen here?"

"Around fifteen men arrived a couple of days ago from Harrodsburg and Logan's Station," Boones' son Israel replied. He's been sitting quietly, listening. He tended to be on the quiet side. Maybe that's what made him such a good hunter.

"Well, that's something," replied his father. "Gives us about sixty men. Still probably not enough to fend off Blackfish."

Those words struck me like a punch in my gut. I knew if we couldn't beat Blackfish, all the men would be killed and the women and children taken as slaves, if not worse.

Colonel Boone looked grim. "If Blackfish takes this fort, other settlements will fall, and Kentucky will be taken by the British. That'll give them a stronghold in the west for the war." His words sounded like doom. "We need to win this fight."

ⅎ ⅎ

On the next day, a lovely one with warm breezes and clear skies, the boys took the livestock to the river to drink, and the women, including me, took every pot, pan and bucket we could find to fetch water. The well being dug inside the fort had still not hit water. Colonel Boone, patrolling with several men, saw the Indians first, coming across the hill behind the fort before dropping into the cover of trees.

The women had returned by then, but the boys were still out with the horses. I heard the colonel yell a warning to them, and Jemima and I went to the stockade to see what was happening. The boys galloped into the fort, driving the other horses, followed by Colonel Boone and the scouts, who hurriedly closed and battened down the gate.

Peering between logs, I watched as the Indians, walking in an endless single file, gathered on the meadow in front of the fort. The British militia came last, their colorful uniforms and flags contrasting with the near nakedness of the Shawnee. We watched as the Indians cut off the tops of our peach trees in a grove to the left. They then made an enclosure for Blackfish by laying the branches on top of a tent cloth strung between poles attached to the trees. All was strangely quiet for a while, until a very large, black figure emerged from the peach trees, carrying a white flag of truce.

A low mumble came from the people watching this. "That's Pompey!" exclaimed someone.

"Who's Pompey?"

"He's Blackfish's translator."

I knew about Pompey because Colonel Boone told about meeting him during his captivity in Chillicothe. Pompey had been a slave, taken in a raid and adopted as a son by Blackfish. Blackfish couldn't have chosen a more frightening figure to carry that flag, I thought.

Pompey spoke in a deep, loud voice, so everyone could hear. "Chief Blackfish has come to accept the surrender of Boonesborough, as you promised, Boone. He has letters from Governor Hamilton guaranteeing you and all the settlers safe conduct to Detroit."

The colonel called on the men to confer with him on a reply. "We want to see those letters," he finally shouted back.

But just then, we heard a voice cry from the covered arbor in the peach trees, "Sheltowee, Sheltowee."

I figured it was Blackfish calling for the colonel, and soon enough, Pompey said loudly, "Blackfish wants to talk to his son."

I heard some back and forth among the men, and then Colonel Boone agreed to meet the chief outside the fort. Men with rifles scrambled to the top of the stockade walls to cover him. He walked boldly out of the gate to some distance from the fort, where he shook hands with Chief Blackfish and other Shawnees. From my perch in one of the corner blockhouses, I could see what they wore for decorations in their hair and thought some might be other chiefs.

They all sat down on a blanket, young braves standing quietly around them, holding branches over their heads for shade. I spotted a red ribbon and wondered if the Indian wearing it could be the one I'd met in the woods.

I couldn't hear what was being said, and doubted anyone else could. The talking went on for quite a while. During that time, I heard a few men in the fort claiming the colonel would betray us and surrender to the Shawnee and the British militia. But they were wrong. It seemed nothing was decided, because after that, the men sitting on the blanket, including Colonel Boone, all smoked a pipe together. Then the colonel got up and returned to the fort. I descended from the blockhouse to hear what he had to say.

Once inside, he showed everyone seven buffalo tongues that Blackfish had given him as a delicacy for our women. I myself was not partial to buffalo tongue, after my capture by Indians, and someone suggested they might be poisoned. "It is not the Shawnee way to poison anyone," said the colonel, and after some brave individuals tasted them, he was proven right.

"So, what did you talk about?" asked Richard Calloway, one of our leaders and Colonel Boone's loudest critic.

He replied, "I offered them some cattle and what corn is left in the field but told them not to waste the food. I also said I had a lot to think about and I had to talk to other officers in the fort. I reminded Blackfish he'd kept me captive for so long that other men had taken my place to command the fort."

I wasn't privy to the long discussion among the fort's defenders after that because they retreated to one of the cabins. I had to wait until we'd finished our evening meal to hear what the men had decided. In the dimness of the cabin's candlelight, Colonel Boone told us,

"The main thing we need to do is delay as long as we can before the fighting starts. That increases the chance the Virginia militia will come. I'm going to try to talk Blackfish into a treaty. Working out the terms will take some time and hold off on any attack. I'll die along with everyone else who voted to fight, but not before I try stalling as long as possible so we might get some reinforcements."

Discussions between the colonel and Blackfish, and then the colonel and the men in the fort, went on and on, back and forth, during the next two days. This gave us time to continue our preparations inside the fort—digging the well and making musket balls—and I tried to focus on the work and not on what might happen when all that talking stopped.

On the second day, Colonel Boone asked the women to walk back and forth inside the open gate wearing pants and men's coats and hats. He said this would make Blackfish think we had more men than we actually did. "Do you know exactly what your father is doing?" I asked Jemima, as I passed her wearing Israel's coat and his hat.

"Stalling." And when we passed each other again, she said, "It seems the men are split, half for surrendering, half for fighting and dying."

My stomach clenched. Each time I got to the gate, I could see the Indians, their fearful paint and markings promising our violent end. Some of the women, braver than I, made numerous trips to the river through the back gate, filling empty vessels with water. Our well still wasn't deep enough.

At midday, Pompey came up close to the gate and yelled, "Blackfish and his men want to see your women."

Colonel Boone, who stood talking to men just inside, called back, "Tell him that ain't going to happen. Some Indians kidnapped our women and now they're very afraid of you."

"Just bring them to the gate. We want to see your pretty daughter."

Jemima and I stood to one side of the group of men surrounding the colonel. The colonel left them and came over to us. "Take off your hats and coats," he said, beckoning a few other women to join us.

"But why, Daddy?" asked Jemima. "I'm scared. Why do they want to look at us?"

"They're sizing you up to be their women. Don't be afraid. I won't let that happen. But it'll give them something to argue about."

Jemima and I and two other women did as he asked and stepped into the open gate. We could see Blackfish and Pompey standing about a hundred feet away. *Not far enough.*

"Let down your hair," Pompey demanded.

He is well-named – pompous man. We took the combs out of our hair and let it fall around our shoulders.

Then the Indians walked away, smiling to each other. I shook with fear for a while, remembering my time as their prisoner and their harsh treatment. Then our men became angry, some yelling they'd kill Pompey if he came near the fort again. But that evening he did approach us again, although keeping a good distance, and asked the colonel to meet with Blackfish one more time to discuss the surrender.

To which Colonel Boone replied, "We ain't surrendering as long as there's a man here still living."

Blackfish himself replied, "Then let us talk more, together with the chiefs of all our Shawnee villages."

Seeing the nods from the men gathered at the gate, Colonel Boone replied, "We're grateful for this proposal, but I'll bring our own leaders with me."

They agreed to meet the following day. That night, the colonel asked the women to prepare food so the treaty session could begin with a meal for the Indians. To soften them up, I think. So, in the morning, we cooked venison, buffalo meat, green corn, and vegetables we'd collected earlier from our gardens, and added some bread. As Jemima and I did this, we complained under our breaths that they'd eat a lot of the food meant for us. "Why should we feed them, Colonel?" I asked when he came to the cabin.

He chuckled. "Just more foot dragging. Might put them in a mood for a treaty."

Men carried out tables and chairs to the open area outside the fort and put their wives' pewter-ware on the tables. Then we brought out the food. Our guests ate everything, clearly enjoying the meal, while we looked on. When they'd finished, we brought everything back inside. Jemima continued muttering about the waste of food.

I watched as some leaders from the fort walked in a dignified manner to a spot under a great elm tree to resume the talking. In addition to Colonel Boone, the group included Flanders and Richard Callaway, Squire Boone, Simon Kenton, and some others I didn't know that well. I didn't think the colonel thought anything would come of this meeting, because I heard him say to some riflemen, "Station yourselves in the blockhouses and take aim at the enemy. If there be any trouble, don't hesitate to shoot. Don't worry about hitting us—there'll be a lot more Shawnee."

Jemima, being a crack shot, went up with the men. I climbed to the top of the palisade to watch. I became bored, listening to a lot of talking, voices rising and falling in English and Shawnee. Finally Chief Blackfish stood and addressed his army, which had gathered some distance away, and spoke for quite some time in Shawnee. I looked around, and no one seemed to understand what he was saying, including the men under the elm tree. Then he extended both his arms and walked towards Colonel Boone. I thought he meant to embrace him as the end to a peace treaty. But other chiefs moved towards our men, two or three encircling each. Richard Callaway struggled when the chiefs attempted to grab him. And then all hell broke loose.

I remember the first moments of the battle—the fire from our marksmen and the returning volleys from Indians hidden in a hollow near the oak tree. The sudden noise startled me, and I ducked. When I peeked over the palisade again, I saw the Shawnee chief carrying the peace pipe swing it at Colonel Boone and open a gash in his back, blood quickly soaking his shirt. The men all managed to free themselves from the Indians' holds, possibly because Blackfish had hit the ground. I think the other Indians got distracted, thinking he'd been shot. Our men raced back to the fort, rifle fire from both sides continuing. Squire Boone took a ball to his shoulder which knocked him down, but he still managed to scramble inside. One man didn't make it before the gate closed and had to take cover next to a tree stump by the main gate. Someone opened the gate far enough for him to crawl in later that night.

We were lucky those Indians were terrible shots.

When the gate closed, the siege of Boonesborough began.

Chapter 9

Siege of Boonesborough

Colonel Boone later told us that during the last parlay, the Shawnee seemed confident they could take Boonesborough if it came to a battle. "But my throwing Blackfish to the ground made the Shawnee think he'd been shot, which distracted them, and when we ran for the fort, our sharpshooters hit enough of them that we escaped. So now I think they ain't so sure of winning anymore."

Following that first skirmish, both sides fired off and on, but the real siege began that night. The deafening sound of the guns filled my ears —along with frightening whoops and yelling coming from outside the fort. Our animals went wild—dogs barking and horses and cows and other livestock racing around in a panic, raising a dust cloud that filled the fort. Mostly what I remember is the screaming of the women and children, who had taken refuge inside the houses. These sounds made me want to scream myself or bury my head in the dirt to blot it out, but like Jemima and a few other women, I focused on loading the rifles, carrying ammunition, and toting food and water to the men. As we did, the dust from the animals running and acrid smoke from the gunfire stung our eyes and noses.

Those of us with a job to do could almost ignore our fear, but it led to confusion everywhere else in the fort, and we all found the incessant noise nearly unbearable.

Unfortunately for us, the Shawnee and British had taken a position on top of a hill across the river and bullets pinged around us from their firing down into the fort. But they were too far away for their shots to be accurate. At one point, I looked up and noticed one of our riflemen stretched out on the top of a corner bastion. I saw him fire his gun and almost immediately receive a peppering of return shots from the Shawnee. He tumbled to the ground. "Am I dead?" he asked, as he rose to his feet. I would have laughed if the situation were not so dire. Those Indians proved once again they weren't the best of marksmen. I counted fourteen bullet holes in the loose sleeves of his shirt, but he survived unwounded.

At one point the Shawnee rushed the front gate in waves, yelling and hollering, intent on battering it down. Intense fire from the corner bastions drove them back, but not before I thought the end had come and resigned myself to being captured again. Then an unexpected lull followed. We took advantage of it to gather up our courage and resume loading rifles. I figured the Indians were regrouping. Colonel Boone came around to check on everyone at our various stations.

"You and Jemima alright?" he asked, putting his hand on my shoulder. The concern in his eyes told me everything. "You're keeping us going. Never doubt how important you are."

I could only smile grimly at his words, but they gave me renewed energy.

☙　❧

The gunfire resumed shortly after the colonel checked on us, and Jemima and I went back to loading rifles and ferrying ammunition, food and water to the men. At one point, I stopped loading to watch Jemima run from the palisade across the open central area to get some food from one of the houses. I feared she'd be hit and, sure enough, just as she entered the cabin doorway, she flinched. When she came running back with the food, I asked her, "Are you hit?"

"One of those damned balls slapped my backside. It doesn't feel like I'm bleeding, but it's sore back there." She rustled her skirt and her petticoats and dang if a ball didn't fall out. Seeing that ball, we started to laugh hysterically, but some men calling for reloads sobered us up pretty quick. The shot must have been all but spent when it hit her, but when I checked her later, I saw a scrape and a good bruise.

Squire Boone became another casualty that day. I noticed he'd slumped down in pain by a gun loophole, clutching his shoulder. The wound inflicted by the Shawnee rifle fire when he'd ran back from the parlay had required a deep and painful cut to remove the ball. Squire Boone was determined to defend the fort, but the incision now hurt so much that he couldn't lift his rifle. Jemima ran to get his wife, and she had some men carry him to his bed. Jemima told me once the men had laid him on his bed, he'd asked for an ax, in case the fort walls were breached. Bravery ran in the Boone family.

When nightfall came, the firing ended and the quiet scared us almost as much as the gun fire. The children, exhausted from their fear and the noise, fell asleep. That night, men chopped holes between connecting cabins so people could move around without exposing themselves to bullets. Sadly, most of our cattle and horses had died, and some volunteers butchered the carcasses so the meat would not be lost. Jemima and I roasted some of the horse meat and stewed vegetables from our stores to feed the family, running plates of food to wherever they were stationed around the fort. Colonel Boone, when he came to the cabin to check on us and have something to eat, told us, "We can be grateful no cannons have appeared. If they had, this day would've been a different story."

The siege began again at daybreak the next morning and continued through another long day. According to the riflemen, neither side had gained an advantage, despite all the wasted shot.

That night, the men at the palisade reported Shawnee warriors gathering the harvested flax we'd left drying in the fields and spreading piles of it along one side of the stockade walls. When the news came they'd set fire to the flax in order to burn us out, some brave men crawled out under the wall and put the fires out. Bullets struck all around them, and we gave thanks to God when they returned with no injuries.

₧₧₧₧₧   ₧₧₧₧₧

During those first days of the siege, a worn and faded American flag still flew from a pole in the center of the fort, and that flag meant a lot to us. One of the settlers had brought it, a version with alternating red and white stripes and a small blue square in the upper left corner with thirteen stars. It waved proudly in the wind created by all the rifle fire, and the Indians fired at it hundreds of times in an attempt to knock it down. The top of the pole finally broke off, but we repaired the pole and flew the flag again. I heard people say we would die under that flag if we had to.

Squire Boone, whose wound initially confined him to bed, spent the time while he healed making a cannon from the hollowed-out trunk of a gum tree, thinking it would provide us with our own artillery. He wrapped the trunk in iron bands to reinforce it, then filled it with powder and buckshot. After moving his cannon to the palisade, the men opened the gate just enough to let it poke out. Mr. Boone decided to fire it at the Shawnee in the field in front of the fort. The bang and the smoke scared some of them, but unfortunately didn't seem to do any damage. When he fired the cannon again, it exploded in a shower of splinters. The Indians laughed and asked, "Why don't you fire your big wooden gun again? What happened to it?"

₨ ₩

The attacks continued sporadically over the next days, the Shawnee trying again and again to climb over the walls of the fort, but our riflemen drove them back, and some wounded Indians got left behind. They continued to try to burn us out as well. They ran at the fort with burning torches, but the torches made them good targets. So they took to carrying the torches under blankets to hide the flames. Some of the torches made it over the wall, but most landed harmlessly on the ground. Then they tried shooting flaming arrows, and a few did reach the roofs of our cabins.

I watched as one landed on the roof of the Boone house and yelled to Jamima, "Our roof is on fire!" We both raced to the house. A neighboring house blazed brightly as the fire took hold, but so far only a few shingles burned on our roof. "Here, boost me up and I'll beat out the flames," I said to Jemima, knowing I weighed less than she did. I saw women ripping off the burning shingles with poles, but I had no idea where to find one. Flattening myself against the roof to make as small a target as possible, I wiggled over to the engulfed shingles and used my apron to beat out the flames. I pulled out the still glowing shingles as soon as I could handle them, burning my hands. I guess the Indians didn't notice me, for I got down unscathed, although nothing remained of my apron but a charred mess.

I sure could have used one of Squire Boone's later inventions. Tightly wrapping a skin full of water around the barrel of an old gun, he produced a shot of water when he squeezed the skin. This contraption proved useful for putting out small fires.

ॐ   ॐ

Several days into the siege, Colonel Boone warned us that our ammunition was running low, and we needed to take careful aim when shooting so as not to waste balls or gun powder. It seemed the Shawnee and British soldiers had also begun to run out of ammunition, because the firing from both sides decreased. We welcomed less noise but then startled when a shot rang out, breaking the quiet. Running through the open space in the center of the fort still tempted fate.

During this partial lull, one of the men on the bastions noted that the water in the river flowing behind the fort had become very muddy. The river ran pretty close to the fort, but at this time of year, it wasn't much more than a slow stream at the bottom of a gulley about ten feet deep.

"Those darn Indians," Colonel Boone said that night, "they're digging a tunnel through the river bank to come in under our walls."

I didn't think anything more could frighten me after all we'd seen during the long days of the siege, but I found myself fearful again, hearing this. "What can we do?" I asked him.

"I told the men to dig a tunnel from inside the fort that'll meet the one being dug by the Indians from the river. Works already begun. If we're lucky, we can surprise them."

The thought of the Shawnee coming into the fort from under its wall scared many of us, especially when the men digging our tunnel told us they could hear the sound of digging from the direction of the river. And it came closer and closer.

From the rear bastions, we could see Pompey, the interpreter, watching the fort from behind the riverbank. That told us where their tunneling had started. He would pop up here and there, and the men would fire at him, always missing. He took special pleasure in continually insulting our men's courage and manhood, along with telling us to surrender or be killed. Finally, his head stuck up in one place where a rifleman had already taken aim, and our man fired. Pompey's head didn't appear anymore, nor did he.

Our men asked the Shawnee over and over, "Where's Pompey?"

For a long while, the answer was the same, "Pompey is sleeping." This back and forth ended when they finally called back, "Pompey is ne-poo."

"What is ne-poo?" I asked Colonel Boone.

"It means dead."

Our riflemen grew frustrated at not being able to shoot the Shawnee digging their tunnel, so they started throwing down large stones where they thought the tunnel lay, hoping to make it collapse. The Shawnee responded by taunting, "Come out and fight like men, not stone-throwing children." Thus began a series of insults back and forth with our riflemen on the bastions asking, "What are you playing at down there?"

The Shawnee responded, "Digging a hole to blow you all to hell before morning."

"Dig on," our men replied. "We'll dig a trench to meet you and make a hole to bury you." By now the Shawnee knew we were digging, too. Lots of cursing accompanied the insults, which, of course, everyone, including the children, could hear.

⁋ ⁎

We'd been shut up in the fort for days, wrapped in the noise of overhead rifle fire, threatened by the underground tunnel, eating and drinking whenever we could. Everyone was bone-tired, especially the men rotating their watches and digging the tunnel. All of us walked around in a stupor, and no one really slept—just brief naps, when possible. As time passed, supplies ran low, and tempers flared. By the end of the first week, many of us began to believe we couldn't last much longer. We knew the Shawnee and British had vastly superior numbers, but with nowhere to retreat, we could do nothing but fight for our lives.

Our misery lasted through an eighth, ninth, and tenth day.

None of us imagined things could get worse, but then the Shawnee launched their fiercest assault yet. That night, the sky lit up with flaming arrows and firing so intense, it looked like daylight inside the fort. Scuttling back and forth with food and ammunition became doubly dangerous. Thank heavens for the openings connecting the houses.

When I returned to the Boone house on the tenth night, I found Israel Boone, who had come to get some sleep in the cabin, lying on a mattress but wide awake. His drawn face told me he really needed some sleep. "It's so bright I can pick out anything — even a pin," he said, indicating the light outside. "When do you think it will stop?"

He only shrugged.

When I returned to the palisade with water for the riflemen, I saw a large number of Indians and British charging at the fort, carrying torches and howling the most dreadful screams. Their hollering shook me, along with pretty much everyone around me, and my legs, already tired from the work of the past days, threatened to give out. Screams filled the fort in response, from women, children and even the men.

This time a number of their flaming torches made it onto the rooftops and set them ablaze. I watched as both men and women crawled up to beat the fires out, and anyone out on those roofs proved fair picking for the Indians' guns. The torches spared the Boone cabin this time, and Israel slept on for a while, despite the noise and commotion. The torches and the howling seemed to go on forever, but that night a heavy downpour put out the remaining fires, for which I thanked God.

On the eleventh day, we experienced a strange quiet. The lack of noise proved almost as frightening as the rifle fire and howls. Colonel Boone and the family returned to the house, some for food, and others for sleep while they could. We heard occasional firing in the distance, but it sounded farther and farther away, heading north towards the Ohio River and also toward the southwest.

"Do you think it's over, Daddy?" asked Jemima.

"Well, it could just be a trick," he replied. "No one's going outside the gates for a while yet, just to be on the safe side."

We waited…and waited.

"Maybe the Shawnee and the soldiers heading southwest are going to Logan's Station and Harrisburg. I bet they think the pickings will be better there," Israel said.

The men cautiously opened the gates that afternoon. When we emerged, we found the overlooking hill, the field and the peach orchard camp deserted. They'd left, all the Shawnee and the British, and they'd taken the bodies of their dead with them. When I ventured around to the back of the fort with some of the others, we found they had not taken Pompey's body, which lay decaying on the riverbank. The roof of the tunnel from the river had caved in, probably a result of heavy rain the night before, but we could see it had reached very close to the fort.

We'd suffered some losses in the fort over those eleven days— two killed and four wounded—but we expected the Shawnee had suffered even more.

The siege was over. We'd held our own and we'd survived.

Chapter 10

Trouble after the Siege

In the next few days after the siege ended, we searched the grounds outside the fort. We certainly didn't have to worry about material for ammunition—we picked up pounds and pounds of spent lead, the total amount too heavy for even three men to carry. We dug more balls from the logs of the palisade.

We also recovered some livestock. The cows, horses, chicken, and hogs that hadn't been killed or taken had apparently wandered around in the woods and came back to the field once the firing stopped. They looked so thin and poorly. One stubborn old cow emerged from the woods dragging a strap of buffalo hide, tied to her horns. She must have escaped from a Shawnee who tried to take her with him. Some of our gardens had also survived, so we gathered the surviving cabbages and used some of them to feed our remaining stock.

Colonel Boone had mentioned he needed to write his wife to tell her about the siege and our survival. I'd wondered why he hadn't written her before, once he'd escaped from the Shawnee, and I figured she must surely think him dead by now. Even though she was a tough woman, I knew her heart would be full of pain, thinking she'd lost her husband. The colonel never was good at writing. One of his sons had told me while he liked to read, his lack of formal schooling caused his poor writing skills. When I entered the cabin two days after the end of the siege, I saw him sitting at our table, frowning at a piece of parchment paper. A feather quill and a bottle of ink made from iron, oak galls and tree gum sat next to the paper.

"Can I help you, Colonel Boone?" I asked.

"Eliza, did your ma and pa teach you how to write?" He looked up at me from under his shaggy eyebrows.

"Yessir, they did. My ma said I had nice penmanship."

"Then how about I tell you what I want to say, and you write it for me?"

"I can do that!" I flushed with excitement at the thought of being able to do something for the Boones.

After I had him address the letter and begin with Dear Wife, he slowly told me what he wanted me to write about his captivity with Blackfish, his escape, and getting ready for the Shawnee attack. He didn't say too much about the siege, but he did want me to tell her we'd lost only two men with four wounded. And he included his estimate that the Shawnee had lost thirty-seven. He smiled when he told me to write how Jemima had been injured and where, but that she'd recovered. He added that she and I and Israel had fought bravely during the siege.

Then he said, "Tell her I'll return to Yadkin as soon as I can. But first I have to defend myself against a charge of treason, brought by that two-faced liar Richard Calloway and his bootlicking scallywag of a friend, Benjamin Logan." He banged his fist on the table as he said this.

"Do you really want to say that about Colonel Calloway and Mr. Logan?" I hadn't heard about the charge of treason—nobody had said anything to me, but Colonel Boone couldn't possibly be guilty. So, I would have been happy to write exactly what he said.

"No, not that. But they are. Tell her I'm darn angry with the British. Goddam them. They set Blackfish and the Shawnee on us." He banged the table again.

"Shall I write it that way?"

"Yes, you can write that. I need her to know how I feel. Tell my wife I'll see her soon, one way or another."

I could only hope the letter reached her before he did.

When I finished, he signed his name.

₡   ₦

Israel told me a little about how the treason charge had come to be, but his explanation confused me. Something about deliberately deserting the fort when we anticipated Blackfish's attack. How could anyone think that, especially after he saved Boonesborough?

The colonel found the charge very humiliating, and he refused any attempts we made to talk to him about it. I felt his pain deeply, as did his family, and we all walked around him carefully, giving him quiet to deal with his hurt.

Soon after as two members of the militia had come to take him to Logan's Station, where his court martial would be held, we packed up food and clothes to make the twenty-five-mile trip ourselves. "Honestly, Jemima," I said to her as we loaded a pack horse, "how can they do this? After everything he's done for Boonesborough— how can anyone think he'd betray us? If I was him, I know I couldn't bear it."

"Don't let him hear you say that," replied Jemima. "We need to keep his spirits up when we see him—if they'll let us see him."

I, along with all the members of the Boone family here in Kentucky, found ourselves among the many who traveled to attend the court martial at Logan's Station. The place got its name from Benjamin Logan, one of the men accusing Colonel Boone of treason.

The Station resembled Boonesborough in many ways—a stockade with family cabins along the walls—but it was smaller and didn't have the corner blockhouses. This fort was situated well, with Buffalo Spring nearby for water, and it had a grist mill, which meant we could trade for bread.

With limited space for people to bed down inside, the Boone family and many of the people who had come from all over would have to camp in the field outside the station. We'd done a lot of camping during our winter hunts, and I actually preferred eating and sleeping outside. Squire Boone, recovering from the shoulder wound he suffered during the siege, complained of sleeping on the hard ground. Even with blankets beneath him, he still felt pain.

Gossip ran wild among the campers each night. The militia had chained Colonel Boone in one of the cabins in the fort. No one could visit him. He was denied food and water. All of this proved false. The only piece of gossip I thought to be true was that the colonel's accusers had planned this whole thing before the siege. Why else would the officers chosen for the court martial, all from the Virginia militia, arrive only a few days after the siege had ended?

As the day of the court martial dawned, everyone crowded outside the stockade. I stood next to Moses Boone, the colonel's nephew, who had accompanied his father, Squire, to the court martial. While we waited, I asked him, "Moses, Israel tried to explain the charges against Colonel Boone, but I'm still not clear. Can you help me understand?"

"Well, Eliza," he answered, wrinkling his forehead in thought, "there are basically four. One, that he'd voluntarily surrendered the twenty-six men making salt at Blue Licks to Blackfish and the Shawnee and two, that when he was a prisoner of Black Fish, he engaged with him and Governor Hamilton to surrender the people of Boonesborough and have them taken to Detroit, where they would live under British rule…" He paused here, thinking about the other charges. "Then, when he got back to Boonesborough, he took a party of men to attack Shawnee villages, weakening the fort's defenses. That was right when everyone thought Blackfish would attack. The last charge I know of is that before the attack, he took men from the fort to negotiate for peace with Blackfish. He took them out of range of our guns in the fort, so we couldn't defend them."

"No one told me about that. What was so bad about it?"

"People thought he would surrender them."

"That's all twisted. Colonel Calloway really doesn't like your uncle, does he?"

Moses frowned again and spat into the dust. "Calloway has taken every chance to put my uncle's actions in a bad light. He's desperate to prove Daniel wants British rule and he wants Daniel's commission taken away."

"But why? Colonel Calloway fought bravely alongside us during the siege. And he knows Colonel Boone did, too."

"Who knows why? Maybe he wanted to be the leader of Boonesborough. He and Daniel locked horns over everything from the very beginning. And as to fighting well during the siege? He just wanted to save his skin." He spat again. "We'd better go on in now or we won't get a seat."

Indeed, so many people crowded into Logan's Station that many ended up standing every day for the entire court martial. The Boones sat as close to the front as they could, to support their father and uncle.

A long table stood at the front, where the judge for the court martial, Colonel Daniel Trabue, sat along with the jury—six other officers, three on each side of him and all of them in uniform. I remember wondering if Colonel Trabue felt uncomfortable having to preside over the court martial of such a well-known man.

With a gesture from the judge, a young soldier ran off and soon returned with Colonel Boone, who walked down the center aisle between the rows of seats filled with people attending the court martial. Looking neither right nor left, he went to sit at a table off to the side. Samuel Henderson, one of the men who rescued Jemima, me, and the other girls from the Indians, already sat there. Henderson had married Elizabeth Calloway soon after our rescue, so his father-in-law was actually one of the colonel's accusers. I soon learned he would act as Colonel Boone's defender. How strange. Can he be fair?

The heat was high at the court martial, not only because of the different opinions as to the colonel's guilt, but also because we suffered from mid-September warmth. With all those people crowded together, the space soon felt like an oven. Men fanned themselves with their hats, while some women used fans or waved handkerchiefs to cool the air.

The noise from the crowd had risen like the buzzing of bees at Colonel Boone's appearance. Judge Trabue, using a short piece of wood as a gavel, banged on the tabletop, startling everyone into silence, then brought the court martial to order. After he introduced the accusers, the defendant, and the members of the jury, he detailed the charges, and the court martial began.

That day and for several days thereafter, Trabue, members of the jury, and Samuel Henderson questioned various people who had either been at the salt licks or in the fort during the siege. After a while the talking seemed like a whole bunch of hogwash. At first, the Boones whispered softly among themselves when lies were told or something unknown caught our attention. I tried to follow what everyone was saying, but they kept repeating the same stories over and over. By early afternoon, my eyelids would grow heavy and I fell asleep several times. At one point during the second day, Moses Boone poked me in the ribs. "Wake up, Eliza. Colonel Calloway is testifying."

"Mr. Boone's actions at every turn amount to nothing less than treachery and treason. He is in favor of the British government and each of these charges prove it." Calloway paused, pulled himself to his full height and loudly declared, "He should be found guilty and be broke of his commission."

I heard hissing from the crowd with a lot of muttering, but I also saw some people nodding in agreement, which worried me. Can they possibly find him guilty? The penalty for treason is death!

Colonel Boone remained quiet through each day of the court martial, at least when I was awake. When the sun started to set, Judge Trabue would finally bang his piece of wood and announce the court martial over for the day. With the spectacle ended, people departed quickly, tired of sitting for so long and bored at the endless talking. Then the young soldier would return the colonel to his cabin. We fussed at not being able to see him, but one of the soldiers guarding that cabin told us he had plenty of food and water.

At night, the family gathered around a campfire. Moses went out hunting with Israel after court closed for the day and usually brought back rabbits or squirrels, which Jemima and I skinned, adding the meat to a stew bubbling in a pot hung over the fire. The smell from other cooking fires filled the night air, along with people's voices. On the second night, Jemima asked us, "How do you think today went? Do you think they'll find him guilty? Colonel Calloway was sure angry, and he had a pile of evidence, even though we know he twisted it."

Israel grunted. "He spoke a pack of lies."

"But I saw people nodding and agreeing with him," I replied.

"Let's wait and see what Daddy says when the time comes." Jemima smiled. "He's a great talker."

On the last day, the court finally called Colonel Boone to answer questions and have his say. He refused to sit in the chair set in front of the judge and jury table but chose instead to stand and address the officers from where he'd been sitting. He had to answer an endless repetition of questions, some of which I could tell angered him because he stiffened and his face froze in a fierce gaze at his questioners. When Judge Trabue allowed him to make a final statement, he turned to face the crowd, which had hung on his every word. He spoke plainly, saying, "I'm glad to have the chance to explain to the court and everyone here why I done what I done. I surrendered the men at Blue Licks to keep them from being killed and to keep the Shawnee from going to Boonesborough. They'd wanted to attack right away, but we all knew that the fort was in poor shape and the Indians would have captured it easy. After we trekked to Chillicothe, I had to figure a way to keep them Indians and the British from trying to take the fort. So I made up tales to fool them. About how Boonesborough would surrender peacefully in the spring, and I could talk the folks there into it.

"Then I had to escape. Which I did. I got back to Boonesborough and helped the fort get ready for the attack." He paused, wiping his brow with his hand before continuing. "As far as my leadership goes, the outcome of the siege makes that plain. And all that talking with Blackfish and the Shawnee before the siege was meant to delay them, buy us some time to increase our readiness. Hoping the Virginia militia would arrive to help us. Which they never did." He scowled at the members of the jury.

"You know me. I ain't no coward and I didn't commit treason. And I would give my life for any of them people I fought with. That's all I have to say."

Buzzing from the crowd increased, and some man called out, "You tell them, Colonel Boone!" accompanied by some clapping.

When the colonel returned to his seat, the judge banged his piece of wood and announced, "These officers and I will now retire to deliberate on a decision." They went to talk by themselves inside a cabin on the far side of the open area inside the fort. While they were gone, the air seemed to crackle with lightning, but Logan, Calloway and Boone sat quiet, looking at nothing in particular.

I don't think more than a few minutes had passed before the judge and the officers of the jury came back with their decision. The officers sat and Trabue stood. "This court martial has decided in Colonel Boone's favor," he announced. I heard a gasp and then wild cheering from the crowd and the Boone family, and I think I cheered the loudest. I'd never been so happy, not even when the siege ended.

Judge Trabue banged his wooden stick to quiet us. "Furthermore," he announced when the noise had died down, "because of his actions in defending Boonesborough, at this time we advance Colonel Boone to the rank of Major."

The noise level and cheering then got even louder. Callaway's and Logan's faces turned red with anger and they shook their heads, not believing the result, but they said nothing. We could hear the mutterings of some who disagreed with the verdict — like a layer of resentment beneath the cheering — but the court martial was behind us and the colonel had been vindicated.

Colonel Boone came over to his family and said, "Major—phaw! I don't want that promotion. But we need to get out of here now. The weather's still good and I need to go see Rebecca."

His words excited me because I would go with him and see Thatch again!

We couldn't wait to leave, and the family hit the trail back to Boonesborough immediately, covering the twenty–five miles in two days. After quickly packing up for the trek to Yadkin, the colonel, Jemima, Flanders, and William Hayes—Susanna Boone's husband— and I set off. Relieved of the tension of the past month, I practically danced down the trail on the first day.

However, the court martial had taken a terrible toll on the colonel. He spoke little on the trip, other than some comments on the hunting and mentioning once how humiliated he'd felt. Most of the time, he seemed deep in thought. I hoped his pain would ease with time and with seeing Rebecca and the children again.

He never spoke to Colonel Calloway again. A year and a half later, Indians killed and scalped him. But the Calloway family bore resentment to Colonel Boone for many years afterward.

Chapter 11

Would We See Kentucky Again?

The trek to the Yadkin valley with Jemima, Flanders, William Hays, and Colonel Boone took a couple of months to cover the 250 miles. The weather stayed fairly mild for most of our trip, the trees all fiery with yellows, red and oranges, with the crisp, chilly nights telling us winter was coming. We killed game along the way to feed ourselves and saw only a few signs of Indians. But even when sitting together by the fire of an evening or just moseying along, the colonel stayed quiet. I knew any other time, he would have enjoyed his surroundings and hunting, telling tales of his adventures, but now his usual spirit had been laid low by the memory of the court martial. When we drew close to Yadkin, our excitement grew with thoughts of seeing the Boone family again. I felt a lightened heart because I would soon be with Thatch, and William looked forward to seeing his wife Susannah, who he had sorely missed. Even Colonel Boone became more talkative, saying how happy he'd be with Rebecca and the children again.

Since the colonel hadn't received a letter from Rebecca telling him of her whereabouts, we had to stop and ask after her when we arrived in the valley. A settler, recognizing Colonel Boone, greeted him with surprise, saying, "We'd heard everyone at Boonesborough had been killed."

"Well, we ain't ghosts." He chuckled, the first laugh I'd heard since we left Kentucky. "Can you tell me where my wife is living now?"

The settler gave us directions to a cabin on land belonging to the husband of the colonel's sister, Mary. Reaching a clearing next to some fields, we found a tidy cabin that apparently housed a goodly number of people, judging by the clothes drying on bushes and lines around the yard. Colonel Boone called out, "Rebecca! I'm returned." He stopped and rested the butt of his rifle on the ground, leaned on it and took a deep breath.

The door opened, and Rebecca stood in the doorway, wiping her hands on her apron. She hesitated, then walked toward us, squinting her eyes against the sun and pressing her lips into a tight line. "Well, I see you made good time getting here, Daniel. Your letter arrived but a few days ago. I was pleased to learn you weren't dead."

I doubted that was the greeting the colonel had expected and figured things between the senior Boones would not be easy, but my thoughts were interrupted by a yell.

"Eliza, you're here!" A blur of blue pants, a too-large shirt and flying hair hit me with some force. I staggered back, smiling, as Thatch wrapped his arms around my waist and I hugged him back. Then stared.

He's grown so! How is that possible in just six months? I'd forgotten how much he reminds me of Pa with those eyes and that smile! "Look at you! You've shot up like a weed, I swear! I missed you so much. Come and tell me all about how you've been."

By then, Daniel's daughter Susannah had come running out of the cabin to embrace her husband, and Jemima hugged her mother. Colonel Boone stood to one side, looking uncomfortable as his wife glared at him. Thatch and I held hands and walked to a bench outside the cabin to sit and talk. I was happy to move away from the anger radiating from Rebecca Boone. "Tell me about your life here,

Thatch," I asked. "Have you been well?"

"I'm good," he replied. "Mr. Bryan—he's the husband of Rebecca's sister—was right kind to let us stay here. And there's plenty to eat." He paused, patting his stomach. "I go hunting with Daniel Morgan and Levina and sometimes Rebecca, so we got meat for the table. And we got here in plenty of time to plant a garden out back for vegetables. Mr. Bryan has cows, so we have milk and butter and cheese. He's very kind to us. I suppose we'll be more crowded in there than ever, now that you all are here." He finally stopped to take a breath and sighed, looking at the cabin. Then he smiled. "But the cabin is warmer than the one in Boonesborough, especially up in the loft where I sleep. So that's good."

Thatch always looked on the bright side of things, like our pa.

"I'm so happy to see you again." He put his arms around me and leaned into my side.

"Did you hear anything about the attack on Boonesborough?" I asked him.

"Just a few things from people passing through heading east. It scared me. We figured you and Jemima and Colonel Boone had died, and I spent some time crying after you, until we got that letter."

So I told him all about the siege, and his eyes grew larger and larger.

℃ ℂ

That evening, with everyone settled here and there in the cabin and its loft, Rebecca put bread, butter, and cheese on the table. *Butter!*

Cheese! I haven't had them in so long! Then she ladled out a thick stew filled with vegetables and some of the venison we'd brought with us. It tasted so much better than anything we'd eaten in a long time, and, when I'd eaten my fill, I settled back content against the cabin wall and hugged Thatch, who sat beside me on the floor. "You've been eating pretty darn good, I see," I commented, poking him in his ribs.

"Yup. It's so much better than at Boonesborough. Do you think we'll go back? Rebecca doesn't want to."

"I get that feeling," I replied. Husband and wife had hardly spoken a word since we'd arrived.

Over the next few days, the air between Colonel Boone and his wife grew even colder than the dropping temperatures outside. It wasimpossible not to hear them talking about returning to Kentucky, and their conversations became what the colonel liked to call his 'difficulties.' "An account of these," he told me one day in frustration, "would swell a volume."

He would begin by saying something like, "You know I consider Kentucky our home, Rebecca. Not so much Boonesborough—I'm done with that place. But we can homestead there, somewhere away from the fort and on our own land. The Virginia government gave me four hundred acres of land free and clear, for just us."

And Rebecca would always answer, "Why on earth do you think I'd want to go back, Daniel? We had three hard years in Kentucky, and we lost our oldest son to the Indians. We survived that Indian attack some years ago, and I figured when I came here that I'd be a widow woman with a passel of children to raise. I'm not looking for no more hardship in my life, and the sooner you accept that, the better off you and me will be."

Then the colonel would reply, "But things will be better. The children are mostly grown, and our girls will marry good men who also think of Kentucky as home. We've got land, and if we make improvements—a cabin, some acres farmed—we can get another thousand acres."

I noticed he used the term 'we' and I wondered if in private she'd really put her foot down. Then I overheard another hurt that had turned Rebecca against her husband.

"There were some saying you took a Shawnee wife when you was adopted by Blackfish and lived happy by all accounts."

The silence that followed almost convinced me it was true, but the colonel stood up from where he was sitting and said, "If you believe that, wife, then you can't have trust in me. I have been your faithful husband since the day we married." And he stalked out of the cabin.

₯₰

Their back-and-forths continued, with Colonel Boone not moving an inch. Rebecca occasionally seemed to waver, but Mr. Bryan and his family were Tories and backed the British. I listened carefully when they filled our ears about the foolishness and certain disaster of backing the rebels, as the Bryans called them. But I remained unchanged in my opinion, having helped to fight off British soldiers in the siege of Boonesborough.

The colonel wasted no time seeking people to go back to Kentucky with him. During the spring and summer, he made the round of settlements in the Yadkin Valley. I went with him many times and saw his excitement about the Kentucky territory, his eyes all lit up and his gestures grand and moving. And, of course, he was already pretty famous, so plenty of people wanted to hear what he had to say. He told people how they could buy something called Virginia treasury paper they could trade for land in Kentucky, much more than they had in Yadkin. Soon enough, he'd talked many men and families into making the move.

One evening, we all sat outside enjoying the last of the day. Colonel Boone started in again with Rebecca, but this time his argument was not personal and not really directed at her. "Have you heard about what's happening in Georgia and South Carolina?" he asked. Most of us shook our heads. Just then Rebecca returned from corralling four-year-old Jesse, and the colonel looked at her as he clarified. "The Revolutionary War has moved south. There've been military campaigns down this way and when I've been out there talking to folks, I'm finding their feelings on the war are running high and are darn near to dividing us."

"Your sister and her husband said some of the local people have been outright hostile to them," Rebecca said. "Told them they were going to run them off because they're loyal to the Crown. Now they're afraid."

"Just so you know, I spoke with your brother-in-law today. He's decided the threat of Indians be damned, he and his family will be safer in Kentucky. So they're joining us."

Rebecca didn't react to the word 'us,' and I figured she'd finally decided to leave with the colonel. I think her husband had finally worn her down. But maybe the comfort of some family coming with us, along with the idea that there'd be war in Yadkin, had changed her mind. She began packing up later that summer.

Of course, Thatch and I would go with them, but I had another, secret reason for making the trek back to Kentucky—a young man named Thomas Evans. I'd met him while traipsing around the Yadkin valley with Colonel Boone.

"This Evans fella is happy enough farming the small bit of land his parents left him," the colonel had said as we approached the Evans' place. "But I heard he likes an adventure, and that's just what he'll get in Kentucky."

I saw right away that Mr. Evans was young and sort of tall and comely, with nice blue eyes. Those eyes lit up when Colonel Boone spun his tale about Kentucky, but I noticed he looked more often at me than at the colonel. "So, what do you think, young man? Do you think you'd want to make a home in Kentucky?

"I think so, sir. Do you think I could get a thousand acres to farm?"

"Yup. You can buy those treasury papers when you get there and then set yourself up right well."

Mr. Evans took off his broad-brimmed straw hat and ran his fingers through his hair, which I couldn't help but notice was wavy and the color of ripe corn. "We'll, I reckon the war is going to get here pretty soon, so if I can sell up in the next few months, then I'd be proud to travel with you and make a home for myself there."

"We plan to leave in September. That should give you time."

"And you, miss, are you going with the Boones?"

I felt my face get hot and I looked down at my feet, for once having nothing to say with such a handsome man paying attention to me.

"This is Eliza, Mr. Evans. She's been living with us since her ma and pa were killed by Indians. She fought with me and my daughter in the siege of Boonesborough. She is as near a frontier woman as any I know."

Mr. Evans looked at me, sort of surprised. "You were at Boonesborough?"

"I was. It was a miracle we survived." I found my voice, but it came out sounding like a barnyard chicken.

He just stood there smiling at me, and I swear we said something to each other without a word spoken. Marriage for me was still down the road, my being only thirteen, but I thought he'd be a fine prospect.

Mr. Evans found some excuse or other to come to the Boone cabin nearly once a week after that: he needed advice on how to build a cabin, what grew the best in Kentucky, what tools he would need, and if he could bring along a cow and a horse. And he always found a way to spend time talking to me, asking about Boonesborough and my family.

After one such visit, Rebecca sidled up to me, saying, "My, my, girl, I can see that young man is sweet on you. Maybe he's sizing you up for a wife. It's getting near to that time in your life."

I smiled. "You think so? So far all we've talked about is our families, crops, and what it's like in Kentucky." Turning my face away from Rebecca so she wouldn't see the heat in my cheeks, I said, "I know I'm not ready to get married yet, but he might make a good husband in time. He's not afraid of hard work." *And he's pretty handsome, too.*

ₒ₃ ₓ₃

We left nearly a year later after we arrived, in the middle of September, when the trees had once again started to turn. With the warm and sunny weather, our company of about a hundred left in high spirits. I would miss the comforts of Yadkin, and I'd come to like seeing so far over the fields. But I missed the gentle hills and mountains of Kentucky, and Thatch and I would go wherever the Boones went—they were our family now.

Thatch was beside himself with excitement. He had been asked to lead the cow, which made him feel very important. We had six pack horses with our household goods, kettles, and farming and blacksmith tools, plus food and two crates of chickens. Colonel Boone rode a horse and the rest of us walked. Thomas Evans rode near us, and Billy Bryan led a string of twenty-eight pack horses loaded down with equipment and household goods. But there were poor people as well, people who carried children and packs on their backs. Some were even barefoot.

One day, Jemima rode double with a very small girl. All was well until we came to a flooded river. Jemima, ever fearless, cried, "I'm going to lead you across," and kicked the sides of her horse to get him into the water. The horse had almost reached the opposite bank when a floating log spooked him, and he threw both riders into the cold river water. Screams came from the women watching, but Jemima came to the surface sputtering and holding on to the child to keep her from being pulled away in the current. "We're all right," she yelled. Colonel Boone rode his horse after them as they floated downstream and pulled them out. Israel took a swim and retrieved Jemima's horse.

The little girl coughed water, but Jemima just stood there and dripped, saying, "Well, that dunking weren't pleasant, but I got my bath for the month, a nice cold one. But it weren't near as bad as getting captured by the Indians."

Tom, as I called him since we were now on a first name basis, camped nearby most nights. I felt comforted by that because Indians lived along our route. Now our conversations tended more towards what he planned to build and plant when he got his land, what sorts of animals could be hunted there, and the types of food that could be harvested in the wild.

One evening, before we all headed off to our blankets for some needed sleep, Colonel Boone told us he'd be leaving the next day. "I have to get to Logan's Station for the Virginia Land Commission hearing, so I can straighten out our claims."

Rebecca frowned. "Not again, Daniel?"

"I'll be back soon. Israel can lead and Mr. Evans will provide himself if there's trouble."

Tom, who was sitting next to me, sat up straighter. "Don't fear, Eliza. I'll take care of you," he whispered.

My heart skipped a beat.

ಶ   ಶ

True to his word, Colonel Boone returned before long to lead our party of new settlers to Boonesborough. We arrived toward the end of October by my reckoning, and what a sight greeted my eyes. I saw the same hodge-podge of cabins inside the fort, but the fort itself had been neglected since we left and badly needed some repairs. Some of the palisade logs had rotted, others were missing, and the gates hung partially off their hinges. It seemed none of the high-ranking officers who lived there had bothered to keep the place in good order or even clean. One of the settlers who had come from England exclaimed, "This place smells like a London sewer." I didn't know what that was, but it must have been bad.

Once again, Colonel Boone was embarrassed, and he blamed an old enemy. "I can see that Colonel Callaway still regards only his own interests. I'll have a word with him."

Callaway had been one of the men left in charge of Boonesborough, but if the colonel wanted to 'have a word with him,' he was disappointed, since Calloway had left to take prisoners of war to Williamsburg.

We remained at the fort just long enough for Colonel Boone to get the repairs and clean-up started, leaving only when he received word that the Virginia Land Commission had approved his land claim. During this time, he and his sons Israel and Daniel built a cabin about six miles northwest of the fort, where a cornfield had been cleared by the previous owner. We all left to go there on Christmas Day, along with Squire Boone and several other families, their dogs and packhorses. Tom Evans was among this group.

The winter was already cruel with deep snow. The cold penetrated the clothes we wore and those walking had a terrible time of it. As we approached the Boone claim, I recognized it—the cornfield field and a new cabin where my ma and pa's had been! The scene tugged at my heart, and I looked over at Thatch, who walked beside me. His eyes glistened with tears, and he said, "Eliza, we're home."

Colonel Boone dismounted his horse and came over to me, telling me softly," I know this here was your ma and pa's land, but it was forfeited when they were killed. I hope you don't mind that I decided to build here."

"This is the best place you could have chosen," I replied, my own tears starting.

Chapter 12

A Time for Grieving but a Proposal

Family members crowded into the cabin at the place that would come to be known as Boone's Station and quickly started a fire in the fireplace to thaw themselves out. Having so many people inside also helped raise the temperature. Outside, those who had traveled with us and couldn't fit in the cabin because of their numbers, settled as close to the cabin as best they could. After clearing away the snow from the ground, they constructed crude lean-tos of boards and sticks. These dwellings had only a blanket for a door on one side and could hardly keep out the cold, but their owners took care of each other, sharing fires and food.

I remember this winter as one of the worst—bitter cold, with more snow than I'd ever seen before. The ground beneath the snow, where we removed it, felt like iron under our feet. Colonel Boone discussed the food supply for everyone soon after we arrived. "Rebecca, get out those sacks of corn we trekked here from Yadkin. My thinking is to divide all of that equally with everyone. We can hunt, but there's no knowing if anything's out there in this damned awful cold. Anyone who wants to hunt with me can come."

Israel, Daniel, and William Hayes went out with him, but the deep snow made trapping and hunting almost impossible, and they reported to everyone that a lot of game had starved in the cold, leaving few pickings. What they got, we shared with everyone. Some of our livestock died of the cold, which provided some meat, but turkeys, which were usually plentiful, froze to death on their perches or smothered in the snow. We collected them but they were poor meat, having had little to eat themselves. The men did a lot of grumbling about the cold making it near impossible to load their rifles, their fingers numb from the icy wind. We all shared the smallest of food rations for several months. Thatch and I talked a lot about the food we'd eaten in Yadkin, which only made us hungrierWhen February arrived, the colonel came back from one hunt with good news. "There're whole groves of sugar maples nearby, Rebecca, and the sap should be rising from the roots. We need to go out and tap those trees. And I'm beginning to see some game out there."

With the thaw, Boone's Station soon became an anthill of activity. Squirrels, rabbits and then deer reappeared, gradually becoming more plentiful, and the men either hunted or cleared the land to plant cornfields. Women and children collected the maple sap and boiled it down to make syrup and sugar. As I collected sap in the woods one day, I looked up to see buffalo coming out from the trees to lick the sap. They were pitifully thin and starving. I later told Rebecca and Thatch, "I could hardly challenge those poor miserable creatures for the sap. They need the sugar as much as we do."

During those first years, Boone's Station turned into a group of real cabins, surrounded by a palisade with port holes. Having learned from the siege of Boonesborough, the men cleared all the land around the stockade for a good view into the distance and dug a well. We knew we were never safe from Indian attacks.

As many as nineteen members of the family now comprised the Boone household, and Thatch and I were two more. Young Rebecca and Levina, who were now in their teens, still lived with their parents, along with Daniel Morgan, Jesse, Susannah and her husband Will Hays, plus their three children and six orphaned cousins of Rebecca. Israel Boone lived nearby, having married one of the Calloway girls.

So it came as no surprise when Rebecca shushed me and Thatch out the door each day to help Tom, who had finally got his claim for one hundred acres approved. She needed fewer people under foot, and he needed hands to clear his land for planting corn and building his cabin. The combined sweat of Thatch and me went into dragging away chopped up trees and bushes, but the colonel and Israel had to pitch in to help build the cabin. It seemed to me Thatch grew a foot that year and became muscled and brown from the sun. We returned tired each night to the noise and general chaos of the Boone home, which we had accepted for years as normal, but I came to enjoy the calm and quiet of Tom's homestead.

Any time spent at Boone's Station between his hunting expeditions provided Colonel Boone a needed rest, and he always brought back news of the continuing war with the British and various Indian tribes. During one of his longer stays, he told us that Blackfish had died from wounds in a raid on Chillicothe by the Virginia Militia, but the attacks on various Kentucky stations continued with much savagery, mirrored by the militia attacks on Shawnee settlements. We needed to be prepared. I wondered if these bloody back and forth battles would ever end.

One morning in early August, the colonel told Rebecca to pack food for him—he was leaving again. As he sat outside, cleaning his rifle, I sat beside him. The children, seeing the preparations, were anxious about his leaving and had gathered around him. The summer sun, hardly risen, shone on his face, revealing new lines there.

"I expect you want to know where I'm heading," he said. "Even though Blackfish is dead, the Shawnee are still raiding. I've been asked to join George Rogers Clark's army as a scout. Don't know why, I'm old enough to be his grandpa. But I'm going. My brother Ned's going with me."

We'd met Edward Boone, or Ned as everyone called him, and his family several times since he'd moved to Boone's Station a couple of years earlier — he was much younger than the colonel but looked a lot like him. And his wife, Martha, was Rebecca's sister.

We didn't see Colonel Boone again until late in August, when we noticed a man, trotting up the road to the station in the early morning. As soon as we recognized him, we ran to meet the colonel. He looked years older than when he left. "I'm home, for just a little bit," he said to us.

He sat down on the porch, wheezing, clearly exhausted, and called for Israel. "Son, you go get the neighbors. Tell them to bring their horses. I got something we need to do." Rebecca appeared with food and water, and we all waited to hear why he needed to leave so quickly.

"What happened with General Clark, Daddy? Did his army kill a lot of Indians? Why were you running? Where's your horse?" asked Daniel Morgan. He'd become as inquisitive as Thatch.

The colonel grimaced. "We were coming back from Ohio, Ned and me. Our horses carried a heavy load of game we'd killed along the way, and we stopped to rest them in a meadow with walnut and hickory trees. I figured it would be a good place for an Indian ambush, and I warned Ned. But Ned didn't pay me any mind and just picked up some nuts and started to crack them on a rock. Just then I spotted a bear in the woods and followed it and shot it. I heard some shots from back in the meadow and knew Ned was ambushed. When I got there, I hid behind some bushes and saw Shawnee braves standing around Ned's body and one of them said, "We killed Daniel Boone!" They did a lot of whooping and hollering. Ned did look a lot like me." At this, his head drooped so low, it came near his knees, and I saw wet drops from his tears on his pants.

Rebecca had gasped at this news and sagged back against the cabin wall. I went to stand beside her for support, taking her hand.

"What did you do then?" asked Thatch.

Colonel Boone snuffled, looked up and wiped his face on a shirt sleeve. After a moment, he took a deep breath and continued. "I had to run. I tried hiding in a cane brake thicket, but those damned Shawnee sent one of their dogs after me. I had to kill the dog and go deeper into the cane. I heard when those Shawnee found their dog, they up and left. I figured they was just happy to have killed the great Daniel Boone and didn't want to come into the cane break. I ran all night to get back here."

Within two hours, a party assembled at Boone's Station and the colonel explained that he hoped they could retrieve Ned's body. They didn't return for several days, very tired. Israel told me they'd found Ned, but wildlife had gotten to him and the Shawnee had taken his head. They'd buried him near where he fell. On the way back they'd stopped near Blue Licks to kill game for Ned's family, something much needed for his five children.

Over time, the light in Colonel Boone's eyes returned, but he remained quiet and sad. With Ned's death, he had even more responsibilities, what with a family that now included his brother's. And in addition to his work surveying land, hunting, trapping, and farming, he was elected to represent Kentucky in the Virginia legislature.

He must have made quite an impression on the men in the legislature. As he told us later, "All them men wore fine coats and silks and stockings with fancy shoes. And here I come in my rough suit with my beaded buckskin leggings. They gave me some funny looks.

All that jawing and talking bored me near to death, so I went out hunting a lot of the time."

ℰℬ   ℬℰ

Around that time, I'd noticed Rebecca had added some weight to her usually lean frame, and I wondered whether she'd been eating more than usual. It didn't seem so, and as summer turned to fall with the corn high and yellow, I had an answer to my question when Rebecca announced, "Daniel and I are expecting another babe."

By my reckoning, Rebecca was forty and Colonel Boone a few years older. They'd been married nearly 25 years, so this came as a surprise to all of us, although I figured the colonel already knew. He responded with very few words, compared to his usual philosophizing, "Well dang, Rebecca." He gave us a half-sided smile, which lasted for a few days. I did wonder how this had happened, since he spent so much time away from home.

In March of the next year, Nathan Boone was born. Because of Rebecca's age, I'd worried all winter about her eleventh pregnancy, but she never slowed and kept the household running smoothly. One evening, when I got back after dark, I found Jemima sitting on the porch with a small bundle in her arms and surrounded by family members. "Is that the baby?" I rushed up the steps to take a peek.

Jemima pulled back the blanket so I could see the tiny face, with long eyelashes resting on pink cheeks. "Yup, happened today. Momma spat him out like a pumpkin seed in no time at all. She named him Nathan, but not Nathaniel, as we lost that brother."

"How is Rebecca?"

"Go on in and see for yourself."

"Rebecca!" I exclaimed, when I found her standing over the fire cooking something or other. "How are you? Shouldn't you be resting?"

"What, with this passel to feed? Don't think I know anyhow."

"We can do that for you. Go sit outside."

"Hummph. Best get on with my work."

When Colonel Boone returned from one of his frequent hunting trips the next evening, most of us sat outside with various tasks. Rebecca was grinding corn. "You look a mite thinner, Rebecca," he said when he saw her.

Rebecca looked up from her work, wiped the sweat from her forehead, and gave him a loving smile. "Well, you got another son, Daniel. Jesse and Thatch are inside, taking turns rocking him. You might want to take a look."

Several of us followed him inside, where he walked over to the cradle and peered at his son. His face broke into a broad smile as he gently touched the baby's cheek with a rough finger. Then he strode outside and pulled his wife up out of her seat and hugged her. "You've done a fine job, wife. Did you name him?"

"I did. He's Nathan, if that's all right by you."

Still smiling, he swung her around in the air until she hollered and slapped him on his shoulders saying, "Set me down, Daniel!" When he did, they stood looking at each other for a long while, the love between them as real as anything. I hoped Tom and I would still love each other that much when we'd reached their age.

Nathan became the center of attention. He never lacked for someone to hold him or soothe him. The colonel doted on him especially, bouncing him on his knee and playing with him whenever he was home.

❧   ❧

The Boones, along with Tom and the other fifteen or twenty families, now grew corn and tobacco and raised cattle and horses at Boone's Station. Despite our fears, we suffered no Indian attacks, although I worried about the outlying farms, especially Thomas's. The colonel got news about all the raids that did occur and when there was an attack on Hoy's Station, a place five or six miles south and west of us, he told us, "You know, my brother George helped Sarah and William Hoy establish that station some two years ago. The Indians took the Hoy's little boy and the Calloway boy, and some men went after them, but the Indians killed some of the rescuers. They didn't bring back the boys." He paused in sadness. "That raid was too darned close to here."

We remained on high alert for an attack after that news.

Colonel Boone was away recruiting men from the county for our militia when two messengers came to Boone's Station saying that Bryan's Station, a large one that I had seen myself, was under siege by many hundreds of Shawnee, Cherokee, Wyandotte, Delaware and Miami Indians, along with British militia. When he returned, the colonel left immediately with the men he'd recruited to join a large frontier militia going to Bryan's Station.

What happened there, he never talked about in detail. I know the militia followed the British and Indians, who had retreated from Bryan's Station leaving everything outside the fort to waste. Then there was a savage battle at Blue Licks, where the frontier militia was badly defeated. The colonel came home sunken in sorrow. Israel had been killed. The news hit the family hard, especially me. I worked through tears for several days because Israel and I had been close.

We'd fought together in the siege of Boonesborough, had hunted together often, and he'd helped Tom, Thatch and me on Tom's farm.

The colonel left to return to Blue Licks with a burial party.

Rebecca, for the first time since I'd known her, could not bear her pain and lay down on her bed for two days. We went in to see her from time to time, but she just lay there, staring at the ceiling. On the third day, she got up and quietly took up her chores again. We all took turns hugging her, but she shooed us away, saying, "What happened, happened. There ain't no use dwelling on it. I have work to do. The good Lord will take care of Israel."

The colonel broke down and wept when he returned and often when someone mentioned that battle. He blamed himself for taking Israel with him, saying, "He shouldn't have gone, but he persuaded me he could go. I shouldn't have listened to him." In his grief, he seemed older, almost shriveled, and even quieter.

He didn't keep from his duties as colonel of the county militia though, and he made one more expedition into Ohio with General George Rogers Clark and his forces. When he returned, he told us, "Pshaw, that expedition was just for show. It accomplished nothing. The Indians had just moved out, to the north and west. But I did see some nice land near the mouth of Limestone Creek on my way back."

I knew the signs of Colonel Boone's restlessness, and several times I heard him say to Rebecca, "It's getting crowded here. We gotta move." He clearly enjoyed the privacy and solitude of the forest far more than he did people, as he had his whole life. I myself believed he wanted to move away from Boone's Station and its memories of Israel and Ned, and what he saw as his failures as a militia leader.

So the family all upped and relocated to a larger cabin several miles southwest on Marble Creek, near Limestone, and Thatch and I moved with them. This increased the distance to Tom's farm, and I wondered what would happen. Thatch often stayed over with Tom when I returned to the Boones in the evening, and he and Tom became more like brothers. By that time, I'd reached the age of sixteen and was hoping Tom would propose, so it would have been unseemly if I had stayed there as well. I don't know why he delayed — we talked about a life together often enough!

Tom and Thatch showed up at the Boone's on an evening when the colonel was at home. Thatch gave me the biggest smile I'd ever seen when he hugged me. Is something afoot? Then Tom gave me a hug too, saying, "Let's go for a walk." We talked about our dreams for the future, something we'd done many times, as we ambled along, arm in arm, inhaling the smells of late summer – ripening corn, dank earth, and honeysuckle. When we got back to the cabin, Tom left me helping Rebecca with our evening meal and wondering what was on his mind. Then he went to find Colonel Boone and the two disappeared. When I went out on the porch, I saw them together in the twilight along the edge of the cornfield, their heads close, the colonel nodding. But neither said a word when they returned.

Tom stayed to eat and afterward asked me if I would come outside with him. I didn't understand why no one else came out with us. Maybe? He ran his fingers through his hair and fidgeted a bit before stuttering out, "There…there's something I want to ask you, Eliza." He took my hands in his.

Yes!

"Would you…I mean do you think you could…ah heck, will you marry me?"

I looked down at our clasped hands and nodded silently, then looked up at his lop-sided grin.

"I'll make you a good husband. I'll work hard, and I'll try to give you a good life. I'll protect you, and…"

I gently put my hand over his mouth. "I know all that, Tom, and I'll try to be the best wife a man could have. So just be quiet and kiss me."

Chapter 13

A Frontier Wedding

I figured a whole lotta people would look forward to my wedding because the gathering would not involve clearing land, reaping crops, rolling logs, or planning some scouting party. The occasion would just be a huge social event. I had attended Jemima's wedding to Flanders Calloway some years before and had been overwhelmed by all the people attending. I felt unprepared for all the stuff that went along with a wedding, so I sat down to find out from Rebecca what had to be done.

"First of all, dear, the wedding will be here, of course, and all of us will help make it a grand one. We're your family."

I took both her hands with mine, saying, "You and your husband have been my ma and pa for a long time now." I could feel the tears forming in the corners of my eyes and I could see her tearing up as well, through a broad smile.

"Do you and Tom know when you want to have this wedding?"

"In about a month, when the crops are mostly in."

"Plenty of time then. Mostly there'll be lots of cooking. Daniel and the boys will need to do some hunting around that time and me, you, and the girls will have to do a mess of baking.

Now let's think on what you'll wear. Jemima's wedding dress is available, and I can make it fit you."

Jemima had worn a sprigged muslin dress, white with embroidered blue flowers. I had never asked where the fabric came from, but it had to be the prettiest dress I'd ever seen. "Really? I could wear it?" The thought of wearing that dress made me so excited. *I will look pretty in it!*

Rebecca chuckled. "Well, she ain't going to be wearing it again! Wedding dresses in these parts are shared.

"And it'll take time to get in some good whiskey. Can't have a wedding without it. I'll ask Daniel and the boys to start working on that, too. Mmm…we'd probably better send for Wattie Boone—he's a relative of Daniel's and he's been making whiskey around here for a long time. And we'll need it anyway for the run for the bottle."

"I don't remember that. What bottle?"

She laughed. "One filled with whiskey. A group of young men usually begin a race to where the wedding will be from maybe a mile away, but in this case, I'm thinking from Boone's Station. First one here gets the bottle, and they share it with the groom and the other men racing."

"But there's not a real road from Boone's Station…more like a path through the woods!" I could see the men jumping over logs and riding through brush, muddy hollows, hills and glens. "And all so they can get tipsy?"

"Exactly. Makes it a race. And a lot more are going to be tipsy that day anyhow." We both smiled at that thought. "In the meanwhile, we should be thinking on the food."

⅋ ℤ

The wedding took place a month later, in early October—Tom's and my choice because the weather remained mild but the trees made a colorful background. Plus the crops were in.

Reverend John Baxter, the only preacher for hundreds of miles around, or so we'd been told, had arrived the night before the wedding. He dressed in black, as befitted his calling I supposed, but his suit was threadbare and looked green in patches. He'd been eating food prepared for the wedding nonstop since he'd arrived two days before. Tall and emaciated, he looked like he regularly starved.

Tom had remained at his farm, working, while I had been in the thick of the wedding preparations. The wedding felt far off until I saw that preacher. That's when I started to feel really nervous.

Early on the day of the wedding, after a night when I'd tossed and turned, Rebecca and I took a break from cooking and sat on a bench on the porch of the cabin to welcome guests. Word had spread of the wedding, and people had started arriving as soon as the sun was full up, looking forward to a chance for some socializing and fun. They came by foot, on horseback, in carts or wagons, parking them willy-nilly around the house, along the road, or in the harvested fields. As usual with folk thereabouts, the wagons and carts weren't fancy. The horses bore old saddles, bridles and halters or just had a blanket thrown over their backs, with rope or string serving as a girth.

No one had any fancy clothes, either. Men wore moccasins, leather breeches, leggings, linen or linsey-woolsey shirts, and all homemade. Women wore their best linen skirts or dresses, many of them worse for wear, with coarse leather shoes or moccasins, knitted stockings, and kerchiefs. Still I could see a few fancy buckles, rings, buttons, and ruffles, although they looked like they were from times past.

Most of the women brought food—cheeses, bread, cakes—and the men brought slabs of meat. All of them called out as they came near, "Morning, Rebecca! Is that our pretty bride? How're the young ones? My how your children have growed! Is that Jesse? How he's shot up! And look at you, proud mama of that sweet baby!"

The chattering among the women sounded like a dozen bee hives as they started to lay out the food they'd brought onto tables set under the trees. Lavina, Jemima, and Susannah made trips back and forth bringing the first of the food from the house. The older men tended to fires where they'd set meat from deer, bison, and even some beef to roasting, sending mouth-watering aromas into the air. They jawed with each other, laughing at jokes. The younger men wrestled and chased each other, looking at whatever girl walked by. Children raced around and in and out of the house. And then we heard music, as two fiddlers and a banjo player warmed up.

Finally, Rebecca looked at me and said, "It's time for you to get dressed, Eliza." My nervousness picked up to a gallop. We went into the bedroom, and I put on Jemima's altered wedding dress with the lovely blue flowers. Wearing it made me feel beautiful. Jemima and Levina brushed and twisted my hair and wound some fall flowers into it. "Time to go," they both said.

I took a deep breath and steeled myself to go outside. I hadn't seen Tom yet and wondered where he was. *If he feels like I do, would he be here?*

Just then, we heard whooping and yelling from the front of the house, along with the thud of feet on the porch.

"That'd be the idiots racing for the bottle," Rebecca told me.

There were loud cheers, and we emerged to see one young farmer holding up the bottle to hooting and hollering, which quickly quieted as he passed the bottle around.

When I went out onto the porch, the preacher stood there already, with the male Boones on his right and Rebecca and the girls on his left. He gave me a broad smile and belched, his breath nearly knocking me over. Tom stood ramrod straight in front of him, resplendent in a coat and clean shirt with his hair slicked into place. I let out the breath I'd been holding.

He's here, everything's fine. I took my place at his side.

I leaned over and whispered to Tom, "Don't you dare go getting yourself drunk this afternoon, Tom Evans. I don't want a fuddled husband on our first night."

Tom blushed and whispered back, "Don't you worry, 'Liza. I promise I won't drink much."

I glanced over at Rebecca, who smiled and nodded at me. I needed that small sign of assurance because I didn't know if I could ever be as strong as her, with the endless work of running a household, birthing babies, and taking care of my husband. Especially during the hard times.

When the noise from the yard and surroundings continued, Colonel Boone bellowed, "We're having a wedding going on here, so shut the hell up!" When the noise didn't stop, he went in the house, came out with his rifle and fired it into the air. That did it.

I don't remember anything much of what Reverend John Baxter said, but I remember our vows. I beamed with surprise when Tom took a ring from his jacket pocket and slid it on my finger. "It's my mother's," he whispered softly. "Do you like it?"

I couldn't speak but just nodded, so touched by his gesture.

As soon as the reverend pronounced us man and wife, the men shot off their guns to loud cheering, and I heard, "Let's eat!"

Tom and I just stood there, a little dazed by the commotion, until Rebecca gave us a gentle push down the step, saying "Go get something to eat. It's going to be a long day."

And what a feast it was! Spread out on tables made of large slabs of timber supported by logs set in holes, guests had their choice of beef, pork, duck, buffalo, venison and even bear meat, all either roasted or boiled, along with plenty of potatoes, cabbage and other vegetables. Cheeses, loaves of bread and especially anything sweet, like cake or pie, vanished early. People ate off of old pewters plates and bowls, wooden bowls, or trenchers, using spoons and knives they'd brought just for the eats.

Everyone had their fill although I observed the reverend eating pretty much all day and wondered where he put it. Then the dancing began and went on the whole afternoon and into the evening. I knew it would last until the next morning or until the musicians gave up from exhaustion. We danced reels with sets of three or four dancers, square dances with four couples in a set, and jigs. Solo dancers improvised the jigs, bringing a lot of applause and cheering. There was more cheering when Rebecca and Colonel Boone joined in, managing several dances. Tom and I danced until our legs couldn't hold us up and we had to sit down. Someone else took our place, which happened when any of the dancers tired, so there'd be no interruption of the dance. The dancing only stopped when the musicians needed a rest.

All of this was often interrupted by toasts to me and Tom. A man, usually tipsy, would raise his flask in his right hand, saying, "Health to the groom, not forgetting myself; and here's to the bride, thumping luck and big children." With all those toasts, I expected I'd have a large family.

By the time the sun dropped in the west and the frenzied enjoyment had slowed, I found Tom. "We'd best be leaving, husband. We're going to be picking our way home at least part way in the dark as it is."

We both embraced the Boones—all of them—and Thatch, who would stay with them for the next few days. Tom located his mare while I changed back into what I had worn that morning. I sighed, looking at the lovely wedding dress, fingering the embroidered flowers, and saying a silent prayer for the next person to wear it.

After Tom mounted the horse and I got boosted up behind him by Colonel Boone himself, we made our way down the trail leading from the Marble Creek cabin, to the whoops and hollers and yells of good wishes from the crowd. I knew they'd continue celebrating well into the night, until they fell down drunk or tired. Because we lived too far from the Boones, no one had decided to follow us home and raise a ruckus, as had happened after Jemima's wedding, and that was fine by me.

I leaned my head against Tom's broad, warm back and inhaled the scent of him, sweaty from the dancing but with the fresh smell of lye soap from his shirt. The stars came out to light our way, as the horse slowly ambled along, being careful where she placed her feet. I looked up and took a deep sigh of contentment and wrapped my arms tighter around my new husband.

Chapter 14

He's Still a Part of Our Lives

Tom and I settled into marriage like putting on a pair of old slippers. I had expected the work on our farm to be exhausting, and it proved to be so. But at the end of each day, Tom, Thatch, and I would talk to each other over the evening meal I'd prepared and then head outside in all but the coldest weather, enjoying the birds swooping in the twilight and watching the stars come out. At night, Tom's and my love for each other left us tired and happy.

Thatch was an important part of our family, helping Tom in the fields and keeping us laughing with his sense of humor. I watched him grow from a little boy to a gangly youngster who ate everything in sight and who looked so much like our dad that he often took my breath away.

Our farm made a profit in its early years, which Tom put back into buying more land. At first we raised mainly corn, but later added wheat, oats, barley, and hay. I grew a variety of vegetables in my large garden— beans, beets, cabbages, carrots, turnips, onions, and squash, among others. We raised a small barn for our animals, and Tom fenced my garden, since we had so many little four-legged neighbors that liked the taste of what was growing.

We didn't see the Boone family often, although Tom went hunting with Colonel Boone and his sons several times a year. The meat they brought in prompted us to build a smoke house next to the barn.

In 1784, the colonel became quite famous when John Filson wrote about his adventures in a book called *The Discovery, Settlement, and Present State of Kentucky*, which Tom purchased for us to read. The stiff way in which Colonel Boone narrated his adventures to Mr. Filson sounded different from his telling of them to us, but I had observed that he could match his speech to whoever he spoke to—his family, the backwoodsmen, the Indians, the legislature. And Colonel Boone swore the details of every story were true. Not surprisingly, becoming a hero and a legend didn't change him.

When I became pregnant a few months after our wedding, I called on Rebecca for advice about all the changes going on in my body and to ask her if she would be my midwife. She was the best I knew. When my time came, my poor nervous husband rode like fury to get her, and she came immediately. I delivered our son Tommy in the early hours of a hot August day, with Tom pacing incessantly up and down on the porch.

ↁ   ↂ

Later that day, we all sat outside in the shade, fanning ourselves, with Tom looking proud as a peacock and exhausted, as if he'd given birth himself. Rebecca, all smiles, rocked Tommy, loosely wrapped in a blanket. Thatch leaned against the side of the house, whistling. He'd stayed outside the whole time with Tom, trying to distract him from my cries of pain. I just leaned back in my chair, tired and happy the birth was over but happier yet to be a mother.

"How are you and the colonel doing these days, Rebecca?" Tom asked. "We miss seeing you regularly now that you moved from Marble Creek to Limestone."

"Daniel is providing well for the family, but he's unhappy. He's not hunting much anymore and doesn't get to spend time trekking in the wilds."

"What's taking up all his time?" I asked.

"Well, Daniel opened a tavern at the house, selling meals and spirits. I do the cooking. He's into trading in furs, maple sugar, and ginseng, and he buys and sells horses. He's also working as a land agent, surveying and selling land. Lordy, there ain't anything he's not into. He's always running. And he's got me running too."

Tom smiled and asked, "Is your cabin big enough for everyone now?"

Rebecca chuckled. "No, our cabin days are done. The house is wood frame, built with lumber from dismantled flatboats. Maybe Tom could build you a house like that someday."

Tom looked thoughtful at the suggestion.

"Let's do that," Thatch said. He loved building.

The baby started to fuss, so I took him to nurse, saying, "I expect you're busy as always with all the children and grandchildren."

"Yup, there's always a child underfoot," she replied, shaking her head.

Before she left, Rebecca invited us to visit. "I expect there'll be some weddings soon. Livina and Rebecca are courting. We'd like you there for the festivities."

Tom, little Tommy, Thatch, and I did visit Limestone for Livina's and Rebecca's weddings, both in 1785, by which time I carried our second child, Daniel. We discovered that Colonel Boone had chosen a fine spot for his businesses—Limestone sat alongside a place of river traffic from Pittsburgh and overland travel of people moving west. Who better to give advice and find land for these settlers? The Boone family prospered at last.

However, Rebecca told me her husband had become entangled in conflicting land claims, which threatened to impoverish them with all the lawsuits. His financial troubles increased when he lost a huge shipment of ginseng in a boating accident and got swindled out of ten thousand acres of land.

We had been visiting with the Boone family when Colonel Boone told us he'd decided to move his family again, as the result of a new claim that appeared for his land at Boone's Station. "In years past, there's been a lot of land claims being made, with lots of maps made by different surveyors," he told us. "Nine years back, I mapped a tract of land for James Hickman. And then things got confusing. Hickman hired another surveyor for that land to assure his claim, and that surveyor told me I'd have to relocate, saying the Hickman claim overlapped mine. Now Hickman is claiming the land at Boone's Creek—where we were living afore here—is his, too, even though I moved from my first claim. I think the best thing we can do is move on, before he decides to claim our land here in Limestone, too." He chuckled a bit at that thought. "I'm going to turn my land business over to my son-in-law, Will, and sell my warehouse and tavern. We need a fresh start."

We were all on hand to say good-by to the Boones in 1788. The colonel had decided to move to a place called Point Pleasant, which stood at the junction of the Kanawa and Ohio Rivers in northwest Virginia. We watched in sadness as they joined the traffic on the Ohio River, the family poling their way north on a keelboat holding all their goods.

On the way home, with Tommy and Daniel tucked in the back of our wagon and Thatch dozing beside them, Tom said to me, "Poor Daniel. It seems every business he tries, fails. He's just not made up to be a businessman. Better he stick with what he knows."

"Scouting and hunting? There's not much call for that around here now," I replied. "Plus, he's getting pretty old for exploring."

"Well, I wish him luck. Maybe he's realized his real life lies in the wilderness, and Point Pleasant is still wilderness."

ಶ ೞ

Thatch had met a girl named Rachel at Rebecca Boone's wedding, and he saw her again when we attended social events afterward. By the spring of 1790, we noticed him disappearing most evenings. I had dreaded the day Thatch would marry and move to his own farm but knew life moved on. When Tom told me he would help Thatch purchase land for a farm of his own, it became apparent another wedding was not far off. My brother had never been happier, at least in my eyes, and I thought back to the day our parents died and our frenzied run through the forest, with little Thatch holding my hand or riding on my back. I shed more than a few tears at his wedding, thinking about that and all the years since.

ಶ ೞ

The frontier news carries fairly quickly along the Ohio, and we soon learned Colonel Boone had opened a trading post at Point Pleasant. Seven years later, we were surprised to learn the Boones had moved yet again, this time back to Kentucky, settling near

Blue Licks. We visited him there, where he and Nathan had cleared land, built a cabin, and planted several acres of crops.

We all sat outside the cabin on benches, watching my children—now four in number—chase each other around the yard, overseen by a smiling Rebecca, who had spent most of the day cooking to celebrate our arrival. She looked her age, a little worn with care, but had her usual energy.

"Daniel is much afflicted with rheumatism and arthritis," she told me, as I helped her cut up vegetables from her garden for the meal she'd organized. "I had to hunt with him in the woods outside of Point Pleasant. His fingers are so bent, I had to aim and fire for him. Don't mention this, though. He's got his pride, and he's still the best tracker I've ever known."

Colonel Boone had put on some weight but otherwise still had a sound mind and a strong stance. He remained the kind and friendly man we'd always known. When we asked why he'd come back to Kentucky, he replied, "There ain't much good hunting left up there on the Ohio, too many people, too darn civilized."

What he didn't tell us was that land disputes and accusations of fraud followed him wherever he went. When they eventually trailed him back to Kentucky, he and his family left us again, moving to the Missouri territory, where there was still wilderness and good hunting, along with Indians. We missed him and Rebecca, but the Boone family stuck together. Jemima, Flanders, and their children, and Nathan and Daniel Morgan, who had both married, went with him.

By this time, I reckoned he must have been sixty-four, probably time to retire from the active life of a woodsman, but I doubted he would. Wherever he could find virgin territory, Colonel Boone would explore it and hunt. We lost track of the Boones for a time after that, except for an occasional word or two brought back by travelers.

Tom and I saw him for the last time in the spring of 1810, when he came to Kentucky to pay some outstanding debts. By that time, we had a prosperous farm – a large wood-sided house with a shingle roof and a large porch, a larger barn, and a number of outbuildings. Tom had hired sharecroppers to help him farm.

We now had six children—Tommy, Daniel, Israel, Rebecca, Susannah, and little Jemima. Washing their clothes took up a lot of my time. One spring morning, as I washed a load of garments outside in a tub of heated water, I thought how nice it would be when Rebecca and Susannah were strong enough to really help me. So far, they'd learned how to put the wet clothes out to dry over a line, which they needed a stool to reach, but they often dragged the freshly washed clothes in the dirt. As I paused to wipe the sweat from my forehead, I noticed a figure coming down the road to our farm. The man leaned on a stout, rough stick. Looking more closely, I saw an older version of the Colonel Boone I had known, a little diminished by age.

"Howdy, Eliza," he said as he approached.

I dropped the shirt I'd been wringing into the tub, wiped my hands on my apron and ran to greet him with a hug. "You're a sight for sore eyes, Colonel."

"I think you can call me Daniel by now. Look at you—still the pretty girl I found at the waterfall."

Just then, three of my four youngest children ran out from behind the house, where they'd been feeding the chickens, curious to know who was talking. They came to an abrupt stop in front of the colonel and squinted up at him.

"Howdy, children, I'm Daniel Boone."

"Really?" they all said together. I thought Israel and Rebecca might have remembered what he looked like, but they all stood there with their mouths open. Probably because of all the tales I'd told them about him.

"Children, introduce yourselves to the colonel." After Israel had shaken Colonel Boone's hand, I said to him, "Israel, go find your father, Tommy, and Daniel. Do you know what fields they're in this morning?"

Without answering me, he sprinted off, his spindly arms and legs pumping.

"Come sit on the porch and take a load off your feet, Daniel," I said a little hesitantly, using his first name. "Girls, you go fetch some more chairs."

When the girls had seated themselves next to the colonel, they began peppering him with questions. I went inside and brought out a pitcher of cool water which I'd flavored with sugar and lemon juice from a small lemon tree we grew in a tub. The children grabbed their mugs before I cautioned them to let our guest have the first drink.

"Daniel and Israel and Rebecca, huh? I'm honored you'd name your children after me and mine. Rebecca will be mighty pleased, too. This here lemon water is real refreshing, Eliza. Never had it before."

"Well, I think we're the only ones to have it, and only as long as the lemon tree survives."

At that point, I saw Tom and our oldest sons coming from the fields, followed by a panting Israel, and I waved to them. Tom broke into a trot, and the colonel stood as he approached. "Tom, you have a mighty fine place here. Looks like farming suits you. You must be doing well." He gestured at the house.

Tom shook his hand heartily, as did Daniel and Tommy, who remembered him. They sat around him when I motioned the youngest to give up their seats. "Yup, we had some lean years, but our crops are doing well, and I've bought more land. What brings you to these parts again?"

"I need to pay off my debts here. And I want to visit with Squire. It's been a long while." He looked wistful.

I took Susannah's chair, putting her on my lap. Finally, I had a chance to take a good look at the man who'd saved me and Thatch. His hair was now gray, turning white, but thick and unruly as always. He appeared solid and muscled in leggings, moccasins, a linen shirt and a blue cloth jacket. But crippled, though, looking at his hands. Surprisingly, his face had only a few lines, drooping of the corners of his eyes, and wrinkles around his mouth. The years seem to lie lightly on his face, if not his body.

Colonel Boone looked around at the children and said, "You got three fine boys here. And two pretty little girls. Are you planning on more?"

I chuckled. "You haven't met Jemima yet…" His eyebrows rose. "My youngest's in the house napping." I put Susannah down and went to fetch her.

"How's Rebecca?" I heard Tom ask.

"Just as mean and strong-headed as usual," he answered. "She's busy taking care of our Jemima's children. She's got fourteen now, so Rebecca's some busy."

"Fourteen?" I exclaimed, coming out onto the porch with little Jemima holding onto one of my hands. "Sounds like one a year."

"You might be right, but you've not done poorly yourself," the colonel said, looking around at my six children. "So this is Jemima. Howdy, young lady."

Jemima, shy at two years old, hid behind my skirt. I sincerely hoped she was my last.

"Dang if she doesn't look like my Rebecca with that dark hair and eyes," Colonel Boone remarked, chuckling.

"How's young Thatch doing?" he asked, while I took a seat with Jemima on my lap.

I let Tom answer. "Not young Thatch anymore, but right well. He has his own farm about ten miles from here and is married himself with four children of his own. His farm is thriving."

"Good to know. I'll tell Rebecca," he said with a smile. "She speaks of you all often."

He seemed to want to talk about old times and get news of the families he knew that still lived hereabouts. He told us only a little about his life where he had settled, on land that had been incorporated into Missouri, or any difficulties he might have had. But he enjoyed telling us about a man he'd met named James Audubon. "He travels around painting—birds, can you imagine that? I went hunting with him—he's a dang good shot. You'd like his paintings, Eliza. The birds look like they're real."

From everything we talked about, we could see he still preferred to be on the road or in the wilds, exploring and hunting, rather than doing what he called 'drudge and business.'

The youngest children and I cried when he finally said he had to be on his way. Tom shook his hand again and I hugged him, giving him a sack of food for his journey. The older children solemnly shook his hand, and the little ones grabbed him about his legs, and we had to detach them. My last sight of him was a figure leaning on his stick, walking a little more slowly down the road, looking around as if savoring being in Kentucky again.

Frontier gossip told us that later that year, he'd formed a hunting party with his sons-in-law and two friends from his Kentucky days to explore the Great Plains and the Rocky Mountains. A last great adventure and at his age! They'd returned to Missouri in several boats filled with furs, with Colonel Boone proudly steering one of them. I could just imagine that old hunter in the splendor of those mountains and his joy at exploring the environment he loved best.

Shortly after this news, we heard Rebecca had died. I felt deep pain at her passing, thinking of all her kindness to me and Thatch, her devotion to her husband and children, and the hard life she'd had. I couldn't imagine how the colonel would survive without her.

We heard no more about him until the Kentucky Gazette published the news of his death in a long and praiseful obituary in 1820. Colonel Boone had died peacefully at the age of 86 in Nathan's home in Femme Osage Creek in Missouri. After reading the piece, which contained some outright lies as well as truth, I spent some time thinking about all of my adventures living with him and Rebecca and found comfort, despite the hole in my heart, in telling more of those stories to my six children.

His like would not be seen again.

AUTHOR'S NOTE

This book began as a short story, written in response to a 'prompt' from a fellow blogger. My critique group liked it and encouraged me to expand on it. Thus began *Daniel Boone and Me*.

Given our nation's recognition of indigenous peoples and the incredible list of wrongs that have, and occasionally continue to be, done to them, I knew the subject of Daniel Boone would be very sensitive—particularly the settling of Kentucky and the taking of land occupied by the people who lived there first.

History cannot be rewritten, but it can teach us.

For *Daniel Boone and Me*, I stuck as closely as possible to the facts of Daniel Boone's story, from just before the siege of Boonesborough to his death and deliberately avoided adding many details of the brutal war that ravaged both the native American tribes and the settlers. I believe to be correct the Shawnee's the fair treatment of Boone and the details of the 'adoption' of those captured by the Shawnee.

When I interviewed an elder of the Mi'kmaw tribe in Maine for the book *The Last Pilgrim*, he told me that most of our country's history is told from the point of view of the settlers, and perhaps someday someone with Native American heritage will tell their side of the story. Daniel Paul, an elder and author of *We Were Not Savages*, has now done this eloquently for the Mi'kmaw.

For readers and students wishing to know more about the Shawnee, they might want to read *The Shawnee,* a book by Jerry E. Clark, Professor of anthropology at Creighton University, or *Blue Jacket: Warrior of the Shawnees* by John Sugden. There are many more books emerging, written by members of the 547 tribes now officially recognized by the US government.

Finally, among the many resources I used to write this book, there are four books that stood out for me in the telling of Daniel Boone's story: *Daniel Boone* by John Mack Faragher; *Boone, A Biography* by Robert Morgan; *My Father, Daniel Boone* by Nathan Boone; and *Daniel Boone's Own Story and The Adventure of Daniel Boone* by Daniel Boone and Francis Lister Hawkes.

ACKNOWLEDGEMENTS

There is always a village supporting, encouraging, and critiquing an author's work, and I am fortunate indeed to have an incredible village. First and foremost is my husband, Gene, who does a lot of the work necessary to run a household with a preoccupied writer and two psychotic cats. He has been, and always is, supportive of all my efforts!

The members of my Early Birds critique group contributed so much to my being able to finish this book: pushing back on my procrastination, helping me find the right voice for Eliza, and making sure the historical details were accurate. Dawn Ronco is my 'voice' coach, the seeker of passive voice, and my English professor. Elizabeth Calwell is my 'emotion' coach for places which lack it, and Denis Dubay is my 'rewording coach' who makes the writing more interesting and eliminates the 'was's.' Finally, Bob Byrd is my firearms expert and my 'romance coach' who can imbue love into any situation. Together, they make an awesome group which slices, dices, inserts, and polishes my writing.

I give special thanks to my editor, Alison Williams, who has been reading and shining up my books since the very first one I published in 2014. She finds the inconsistencies that people too close to the book can't see, proposes ways to improve the writing, and picks up on grammerly details.

Finally, to my publisher, Drew Becker, huge thanks for putting up with my occasional idiocy in formatting the book and some unusual requests.

This is my village, and they are great company.